Desperate Deadline

JOHN ST. ROBERT'S OTHER SUSPENSE-FILLED 5 STAR NOVELS INCLUDE:

1. **GOING DOWN**—First thriller in detective Joe Kavinsky series of crime/ mystery novels

2. **TUNE OF TERROR**—Harmonious detective work is filled with adventure and intrigue.

3. **THE PLEA**—Focusing on a dramatic and terrifying rush to Judgment

Desperate Deadline

John St. Robert

iUniverse, Inc.
New York Lincoln Shanghai

Desperate Deadline

Copyright © 2005 by John St. Robert

All rights reserved. No part of this book may be used or reproduced by any means, graphic, electronic, or mechanical, including photocopying, recording, taping or by any information storage retrieval system without the written permission of the publisher except in the case of brief quotations embodied in critical articles and reviews.

iUniverse books may be ordered through booksellers or by contacting:

iUniverse
2021 Pine Lake Road, Suite 100
Lincoln, NE 68512
www.iuniverse.com
1-800-Authors (1-800-288-4677)

ISBN-13: 978-0-595-37753-4 (pbk)
ISBN-13: 978-0-595-82129-7 (ebk)
ISBN-10: 0-595-37753-X (pbk)
ISBN-10: 0-595-82129-4 (ebk)

Printed in the United States of America

Special thanks to my wife, a dedicated nurse, and family for support and advice. I also appreciate help from computer consultant Janet Winsand and Harry Clark, and my son and son-in-law who taught me some new computer "tricks." I'm especially grateful to the wonderful nun who told me of her thoughts while in a long, deep coma(thanks sister). Writing this novel also helped me recall my own frightening memories of going through a "spinning tunnel" while sedated during surgery. As a work of fiction, however, any resemblance to actual persons, living or dead, organizations, events or locales is entirely coincidental.

Chapter 1

▼

His screaming for help stopped suddenly, along with the terror and panic he felt falling into a deep spinning tunnel. A flickering light at the bottom of the tunnel seemed to be beckoning him downward. But for some mysterious reason, he quit falling just before reaching the light. Everything became quiet, as if turned off by a switch. Even the loud pounding of his heart no longer echoed throughout the tunnel. Until this horror stopped, every movement was a struggle. But he soon realized that escaping from the tunnel led to another frightening, horrible experience. He now found himself on a stone-hard bed, his head sinking into a pillow wet with sweat, and desperately looked about to see where the hell he was.

At first, he saw no one. But upon peering further into the apparent nothingness of his surroundings he noticed a small, slim figure of a woman…standing quietly gazing at some far out object as though in a trance. She was a only a few feet from his bed- motionless and without expression—like a statue meant to simply add a touch of apparent humanity to his unimaginable, depressing surroundings. Although he couldn't see her eyes, he noticed her mixture of gray and blonde hair that made it difficult to determine if she was old or young. She didn't look back at him. He could also see that she was doing something with her hands at a nearby table.

"Who the hell are you?" he shouted, rising slightly from the bed so she would notice him. He saw a phone on a table too far out to reach from the bed. Although he didn't know who to call, he vaguely remembered some emergency phone numbers he had placed on the table.

I'm talking you lady, damn it!" he screamed again demanding the attention of this silent, mysterious female.

She looked away at first, but then returned his stare with a cold stare of her own. Her eyes seemed blank and, without a word spoken, she began to walk slowly toward him. He now could see she was much younger than the color of her hair indicated. But his curiosity changed quickly to fright once more as the unsmiling figure came closer to the bed.

"Who the hell do you think you are? Answer me!...I'm Al Benjamin, a reporter for one of this city's biggest newspapers. Can't you see I want your help?. I can't move, I need to call someone! What's happening to me? Please say something...anything. Are you alive, or am I dead?" he bellowed, pleading for her to acknowledge his dilemma.

"You're dead," declared the woman solemnly, as she grabbed a pillow from another bed. Frightened beyond words, he couldn't yell any longer as she placed the pillow over his face. He could only gasp for air as he once again began falling down that terrible tunnel.

In a desperate effort to save himself, he tried to fight his attacker by raising his hands up and flailing them about while unable to move from the bed. His hands, however, accidentally struck the table, causing the phone to crash on the hardwood floor and emit a loud and continuous busy sound. It's beeping could still be heard once the struggle ended.

Chapter 2

While all this drama was unfolding in Al's mind, his wife Kay was frustrated being unable to contact her husband at the hospital. She tried phoning him many times but could only get a busy signal. She knew he couldn't be using the phone since he could hardly move after such surgery. Having a bad case of the flu, all Kay could do was call her nephew for help.

* * * *

"Joe-Joe Kavinsky!—your aunt wants you on the phone," my secretary shouted, somewhat startling me while reading a crime report. My 'sixth sense' seemed to be already alerting me that my uncle may need assistance. Being a cop, I came to respect that feeling…the kind you get sometimes that someone, somewhere requires immediate help. It's tough to explain, but I suppose it's from my strange experiences with the criminal world. At first I simply shrugged it off, but couldn't help feel this was something special…making me somewhat guilty for not visiting Al at the hospital more often where he was recovering from surgery to fix a longtime shoulder injury. His rotator cuff bothered him since his days as a GI in the Korean War. But, like my aunt, I was informed by his pre-op medical report that surgery would be safe and easy.

Seemingly disturbed, Kay told me she still couldn't reach Al on the phone. To help, I tried calling his room first but only got a busy signal. I tried again…still nothing. I then called Kay back who urged me to keep trying. I finally phoned the hospital directly. After another long wait someone answered, a busy receptionist I presume. I asked to be contacted to his room—but after more longtime waiting I was surprisingly informed that there was no Al Benjamin listed and, of course, no phone number for him.

Wondering what the hell's going on—I then called aunt Kay back. She informed me that perhaps Al had just been moved to a rehab clinic and suggested that we both try to reach the hospital's patient information department. When I did, I was told he had been taken from the hospital to its nearby center for patients needing further therapy. While pondering all this, and waiting for my aunt to call back with new information, I decided to call the rehab directly.

It took only a few rings to get a human response, relieving my anxiety thinking it would probably be a mechanical voice putting me once again on hold to hear some background music. It also was a much friendlier voice than the one at the hospital.

"Would you please call Al Benjamin's room for me? I understand he was just transferred to the clinic," I almost begged the voice at the other end, assuming it belonged to someone acquainted with the whereabouts of bedridden patients. To be more authoritative, I inserted, in my most commanding way, "I'm detective Kavinsky of the police department and it's very important that I contact him right away."

Figuring it would then take only a minute or so to connect with my usually chatty uncle, I was left holding the phone for all of ten more minutes. Checking my watch to make sure I wasn't late for a meeting with the chief at my precinct, where I've worked for what seems a lifetime, I began to get more impatient and annoyed by such an apparent lack of public relations displayed by the rehab staff.

In fact, I was all set to hang up when finally another voice hopefully came to my rescue. It was different than those I had talked to previously, thank God.

This time it was a man's voice, rather tough sounding for anyone helping patients, I thought. "What do you want?" he asked gruffly.

"My uncle...Al Benjamin. I was told he's at your rehab." Again I was put on hold. But this time it was only for about five minutes.

"Sorry—but his phone's out of order." Getting somewhat bewildered as well as frustrated by all this, I then asked: "Is there a nurse or doctor I could talk to about his health?"

"Not right now. I'm the only one on duty and I gotta go now...there's too many calls coming in." That was it? He hung up abruptly, without allowing any more questions.

I immediately called Aunt Kay back, at least she always had time to talk to me. "What's going on in that place—where the blazes is Al?"...As if she knew where her husband was at all times.

"I haven't the slightest idea, as you know I've been trying to get through to him, too."

Attempting to piece this strange puzzle together, about the only thing I could think of at this point was to rush to that damn rehab center, though not knowing for sure where it was exactly, to see first hand what the hell was going on with my 67-year old uncle.

Nervously racing my fingers though a bulky Twin Cities phone book to spot the address took lots of valuable time, knowing I was probably already late for the chief's meeting. But I figured the best way would be to call that darn center again, realizing my computer could probably come up with a detailed map—if only I knew more about the address and correct name.

But this time, to my surprise, a very polite receptionist responded and quickly gave me the fastest route to take.

With this information, I dashed to the precinct's squad-car fleet, took the first squad I met and sped to the rehab rather than taking my slow car. Although breaking a few speed limits, I figured no one would dare stop me. In fact, I was almost prompted to turn on both my siren and flashing lights. Even though I pushed the gas pedal nearly down to the floor, I still was slowed too often by drivers who couldn't care less about crowding the fast lanes. Honking the horn at some of the slower ones also didn't seem to help.

If I wasn't in such a hurry, I would have given one particular slow driver in my way—an apparent wise ass—a ticket for giving me the finger as I approached the rear of his car in my haste to pass. When I did, I could see he was a teenager with a smiley sneer, boldly returning my stare as though daring me to pull him over even though I'm a cop. However, my attempt to get there fast ran into lots of other problems. Seems the gal who gave me directions didn't consider all the road work going on between the route suggested and the hospital area.

I cursed during this 'race', while encountering a long detour and unforeseen barricades.

Chapter 3

▼

However, at this same moment, Al—although motionless in bed—thought he was in another type of race. It was much more serious as he hurriedly ran down several flights of steps of the rehab building to its exit doors in his hurry to get outside. His hands still shook from pushing the pillow from his face in the desperate struggle with his would-be assailant and striking her with the phone he picked up from the floor.

Once outside, he continued to run through a spacious parking lot until becoming so exhausted he had to stop to catch his breath. When he did, a crowd of onlookers began staring at him—like the same awful stare the gal in the rehab gave him before trying to smother him. They also looked unfriendly, even after he explained what happened.

In this weird setting, Al thought he knew one of the onlookers—a chubby, jovial guy he met so long ago that Al at first couldn't recall his name. Nearly out of breath, he stopped running to get closer to this guy. My God, he thought, it sure looked like someone who attended his old grade school years ago. But it couldn't be... that was back in the '40s. But then again, the face and expression of this fella was a dead ringer for his old classmate George Walling.

"George, my old study buddy—how great to see you. I'm sorry I look so terrible... but I couldn't get dressed fast enough to run off from that damn rehab

building. You wouldn't believe what I've been going through." He added, "How you doing?" although knowing George looked rather ghostly.

But George didn't respond. And Al suddenly realized why—he wrote George Walling's obituary for the newspaper several days ago.

"Didn't you just di-?..." Al couldn't finish his question, noticing that all George could do was stare blankly at him. To avoid staring back, Al looked about to notice the people roaming around the parking lot. About all he could recognize, however, was the dead look they all gave him while passing by, until someone tugged at his arm. He noticed it was a small fat guy who was actually doing more than walking. He appeared to be opening the trunk of a car.

Leaving George, Al approached the guy at the car slowly since he could barely stand upright due to the dizziness he still felt from the treatment he received during his stay at the hospital and rehab. About all he could think about was how powerful those treatments must have been. When he met this stranger, the weird looking guy was busy staring at items in the car trunk as though counting each one…

"Hi—I'm Al Benjamin. Perhaps you've read some of my stories in the Star recently," was Al's opener. "Getting no reply, he added, "and who are you?"

"Yeah, I know who your are," was all the stranger said, in an unfriendly way. He seemed hesitant at first to communicate, and Al wondered if the guy didn't really care who the hell he was. To encourage some further conversation, he said, "perhaps you've read some of my recent articles on drugs and terrorism."

"Naw!—but take a look in my trunk. I've got all kinds of top quality medicine for people like you. If you're smart, you'd check these out and go back to your bed to let your doctors and nurses know you can get them all cheaper from me—right here in this parking lot."

This strange, boastful medicine man then began to find pills similar to the kind even Al was taking. Carefully showing each one to the surprised Benjamin, he said, "Here, take some, you don't have to pay me right now. I'll be back to see you later."

"But who are you? How can I send you payment?"

"You won't find me...I'll find you," shrugged the smiling pill hawker as he slammed the trunk shut.

Al knew he also had to return to where he came from. But where was that? And how can he return?

While trying to answer that question, he almost stumbled looking about to find any familiar place that might help guide him. His legs felt wobbly and unbalanced as he almost inched his way to where he may have begun his experience in this huge and strange parking lot.

He finally noticed something familiar—a big building. For some reason he knew he belonged there...that a bed was waiting for him—as well as some people very anxious to see him.

Chapter 4

▼

"He's really out of it, isn't he?" was all I could say while gazing at my uncle, so still and hardly breathing in the hospital bed. His skin was extremely pale and his perspiring so great that the bed sheet and pillow were almost wringing wet.

"Yes, he's in a very deep coma," responded the nurse at his bedside. "It's typical, however, for someone after such surgery and still under narcotics," she continued as though trying to comfort me.

"But this was supposed to be a minor operation, just for some shoulder repair. No one told me he was going to have such a tough time recovering."

"We're keeping a close eye on him, Mr. Kavinsky. Sometimes it takes longer to snap out of it, especially depending on the anesthesia used."

"Who gave that to him?"

"I believe it was Dr. Frenole. He's with a group of doctors assigned to our hospital."

"Well, I think I'll give him a call. I sure don't like how my uncle looks. I've never seen him so lifeless."

"Keep in mind he's still considerably sedated," the nurse emphasized.

"As a cop, I've seen lots of people in hospitals, miss, including those on narcotics, and I'd say my uncle almost looks like he's been overdosed."

"I suggest you talk to the doctor about that. I wasn't aware that your uncle was on drugs," said the nurse in a surprisingly haughty and defensive manner.

"He wasn't—and he never has been. That's why I'm wondering what happened to him to be in this sad shape." The nurse began to move toward the door, reaching for a stethoscope on a nearby table. Before she could leave, however, I quickly asked "How do I contact this doctor Frenole?"

"I'll let him know you want to see him," she replied somewhat nervously, looking at her watch, as though indicating she had to see other patients.

Realizing there was a big shortage of nurses these days, I continued to stand by my uncle, feeling his forehead and looking at the bedside devices monitoring his heart rhythm and breathing. The pulse readings were sub normal, I figured, and each breath Al took seemed to be a great effort. I also wondered, with all the high-tech beeping devices around him, why my uncle's shoulder wasn't even bandaged or why there wasn't anything—even like a sling—that remotely might relate to his so-called shoulder surgery.

"You wanted to see me?"

The commanding tone of that voice almost startled me. When I saw where it was coming from I quickly realized this guy must have been just around the corner to get here this fast.

"I'm doctor Frenole, and you are...?", asked the bespectacled man in the lab coat.

"Detective Kavinsky doc...the nephew of this patient."

Frenole walked slowly over to the bedside, peered down at Al, grabbed his wrist and checked his pulse. He then studied the monitors for awhile and finally said, "Your uncle is recovering from the anesthesia. but he should be coming out of it sooner."

"Is this normal?" I asked, scratching my head over how dead-like my uncle seemed.

"Well, not really—at least probably not this much nor for this long," replied the middle-aged doctor stroking his chin.

"What's next?" I asked not knowing what else to say. "How do you snap him out of it?"

"We'll work on that Mr. Kavinsky and will keep you informed. I suggest at this point you wait 'till we call you. We'll certainly be keeping a close eye on him."

I still thought about what the doctor said in Al's hospital room as I drove to my aunt's house to update her on his health. My mind kept pondering over what I saw and the surprising casual way both doctor and nurse had reacted to Al's apparent failing condition.

"By God, he better keep both eyes on him," I muttered to myself while getting further upset by all the switching of lanes by the driver in front of me and the many red lights being encountered in my hurry to visit Kay.

Even before parking in her driveway my aunt was already at the front door anxiously waiting my arrival. Although I didn't have much to tell her, for fear this could make her even more sick, I tried to gently inform her that Al was still not "out of the woods" and the doctor was going to check him out more. I could tell Kay was still too ill to be with him at the hospital.

"What do you mean 'check him out'?" she asked, her voice trembling.

"He's still unconscious. There was no way to communicate with him Kay. They think he should be coming out of this soon, however."

"That's good to know, but it makes me feel badly why I wasn't over there more often. I had no idea his recovery would be so slow."

"Neither did I. And I also think I should look into that further, aunt Kay."

I couldn't help but think that something was just not right with the care my uncle was receiving. For one thing, why was it up to me to sound the alarm over his appearance?. I wasn't at all satisfied with the response I got. I recalled some of the extreme drug overdose patients I've witnessed in my police work and how the doctors and nurses would work on them almost round the clock to save their lives. But they treated Al so casually you'd think nothing was even wrong with him.

To dig further into this, I obtained the name of the nurse on duty most of the time with Al and contacted her. When I did, she immediately took the defensive as though prepared to confront me. She admitted, however, that he wasn't pulling out of his anesthetic as expected and still seemed to be in a coma.

"But why? My God this was supposed to be just a rather routine surgery. Why is it so tough to snap him our of this?"

She took a few steps away from me, as though surprised by my sudden anger.

"Did you talk to doctor Frenole about this?"

"Yes, damn it, and I got nowhere."

"You surely don't blame any of our nurses?"

Chapter 5

I'm not blaming anyone—not yet at least."

"Fine, if you have a problem I suggest you contact the nursing supervisor. Perhaps you already know that our board of nursing recommends nurses must always report any suspicious activity observed in any healthcare setting."

"And have you?"

"Not yet—but I will if Mr. Benjamin doesn't gain consciousness soon."

Upset by all of this, I left the room and, instead of trying to reach the floor supervisor, headed for the downtown offices of the Minnesota Board of Nursing. Fortunately, the office was still opened this late in the day and I was able to contact one of those in charge, a miss Susan Peabody. I could tell she was getting ready to leave, but after I told her of my concerns for my uncle, she returned to her desk, beckoned me to sit down, and then, surprisingly, congratulated me for alerting her about this.

"We'll certainly look into this Mr. Kavinsky. You know, the doctors and nurses are so busy around that hospital it's upsetting. But they do have lots of cases of addiction and the like to confront these days."

"It's detective Kavinsky, miss. And I know that many hospitals unfortunately are exposed to the frailties of humanity and not too far located from areas of crime and dope peddling. But I checked this place out and it looks like it's in a very good and safe environment."

"It's one of the most highly respected hospitals around our city detective," added miss Peabody.

With that bit of knowledge, I drove back to my precinct still wondering if my uncle was going to survive all this. It wasn't until I arrived at my usual cluttered desk and upon noticing some of my partners idling around the water cooler, that I thought about checking further into the background of the doctor and nurses I already talked with about my uncle.

"Frenole, Frenole" I kept muttering the doctor's name as I approached my best informed associate, Charley McKay, a narcotic cop at the precinct. "What's up old pal?" he said noticing my serious expression thinking about how to help Al.

"Dunno yet," I admitted. "There's been some folks I've just met and wonder if they're really helping or hurting my dear old uncle who appears to be dying in a hospital."

"Wow!" was all Charley could respond. "Is there anyway I can help?"

"Probably not, but thanks for the offer. He's just hanging on over there at St. John's hospital. It's like he's been drugged or something. Been talking to a Doctor Frenole who sort of shrugged it off saying this happens sometimes after surgery."

"Frenole—did you say Frenole…no relation to Frankie Frenole, I hope?"

"Maybe—why?"

I don't know if there's any connection, Joe, but there was a Frank Frenole linked to one of the drug rings in St. Paul a few years back…and I think he's still pedaling his junk."

"Nah—this guy's Thomas. He comes off as a straight shooter."

"Yeah—but I'll bet there's very few Frenole's around here, and who knows—they may all be related."

Although I shrugged this off, on my drive back home I kept thinking about what McKay was saying. As a cop, I recalled many times when something regarded as ordinary sometimes turned out to be extraordinary—and downright suspicious.

In fact, this bothered me so much that I turned my car in another direction—once again to miss Peabody's office. I didn't want to take much more of her time, but I knew that my wife Sarah wouldn't mind me being a little late for dinner in my attempts to help Al.

I was lucky to catch Peabody just before she was about to leave.

"What's the latest on my uncle?" I asked before she could close the door to her office.

"He's still about the same, Mr. Kavinsky. I wish we had a better report to give you."

"The doc says it's just due to the large amount of anesthesia he was given," I noted.

Surprisingly, Peabody seemed relieved by this. I could almost detect a slight smile.

"At least he didn't infer it was the fault of one of our nurses." She responded.

With that, she returned to her office door, opened it and welcomed me in. Sitting back on her desk chair, she reached down and opened a drawer that seemed full of official papers.

"Just so you know our nurses have special guidelines to protect patients during care and recovery Mr.Kavinsky, I would like to show you the strict requirements the board emphasizes to our nurses should they encounter any questionable matters relating to patients, both comatose and otherwise and how they can detect and report this."

I sat down on the chair facing her desk, figuring this may take some time considering the large file she was holding.

At this point, she began reading the rules for nurses to follow and any signs of suspicious activity they should look for, especially regarding matters relating to preventing overdose deaths. She called these "Red Flags."

"Excuse me miss, but are you saying my uncle may have been overdosed?" I interrupted.

"At this point, I'm not sure. What I am saying is that our nurses shouldn't always be the first ones questioned if and when this happens." She then began reading out loud the required guidelines issued to nurses for reporting any incident they believe to be questionable.

"It clearly states that nurses in all healthcare settings who observe patient care have an obligation to report suspicious activity of any kind. If there is any question or any doubt in a nurse's mind, the suspicious activity must be looked into further."

"How do you know who to suspect?" I asked, interrupting this bespectacled head nurse who was now frowning and looking at her watch.

Raising her hand to halt further questions, and looking a bit annoyed, she continued, "Investigators have pinpointed red flags that signal suspicious activity among medical workers. They've offered the following suggestions." She then reached for more papers on her desk, as I began to look at my watch.

Reading from a list, she noted: "In a memo also from the National Council of State Boards of Nursing, all nurses, both RNs and LPNs are reminded to focus on suspicious behavior by asking: Does a patient's risk of harm appear to be significantly greater when treated by someone who seems uncannily accurate in predicting the patient's demise?"

She began reading faster, apparently to avoid being interrupted again by me.

"Another red flag to ask is: Were patient deaths unexpected by staff or family? and was the family at the patient's bedside? Another one is, does the suspect often continue patient care during investigation, and removed only after allegations become public knowledge?"

She hesitated for a moment, cleaning her glasses with what looked like a small embroidered hanky and then continued: "Be aware that suspects are often charming and friendly, yet have difficulty with personal relationships; they insist the patient died of natural causes and never show remorse for victims, and finally—do other patients complain about the suspect but their comments are often ignored?"

With that, Peabody sat back in her chair, removed her glasses again and appeared to sigh in relief by concluding these red flag reminders.

"Whew, is right," I remarked, expressing my thanks for her going through all this.

I then leaned forward in my chair, looked her sternly in the eyes, and remarked, "What you're saying is with these rules it would be quite difficult to pin the blame on the nurse."

I then stood up and almost pounded on her cluttered desk, saying: "Then by God who the hell should we suspect? I only know my uncle may be dying on that bed by now and no one seems to know the reason for his coma."

Chapter 6

Startled somewhat by my sudden burst of temper, Peabody pulled back in her chair but quickly regained her composure and tried to calm me with words of more advice.

"I realize what you're going through Mr. Kavinsky, and only wish I knew the answer of how to wake up your uncle. Believe me, we're looking into this. I just don't want anyone to rush to judgement about how this happened."

She rose from her chair, indicating our discussion was closed, and said with a comforting smile, "I don't think at this point we know if there is any blame…or anyone to blame."

My parting words were: "Well, I only know you can't blame my poor uncle. He despised drugs and would never be hooked on them. My aunt could hardly make him take his pills if he needed them. This is probably why he was such a newspaper crusader against crime involving drugs."

With that, I headed toward my uncle's hospital room in the adjoining building to once again see him before driving home to my beautiful wife and child, whom I assume were wondering why the hell I was so late for dinner.

Although there was a "Do Not Disturb" sign on Al's door, I quietly entered and approached his bed. He still seemed lifeless, no indication of any change and still death like.

After looking for a few minutes at the comatose body of my uncle, I said a brief prayer for his recovery, and then reached out to pat his motionless hands as a sign of encouragement and to let him know I was around to help, although realizing he was somewhere else…but God only knows where.

However, one of his hands looked like it was injured. It had a bad cut and was black and blue. I looked closer and by God-it did seem stained with blood.

I was further startled when the lights in the room suddenly went on. A nurse entered with a somewhat surprised look and frown over seeing me there despite the sign on the door.

"He needs as much rest as he can, and shouldn't have any visitors," she scolded.

I couldn't help but notice her hair, it was somewhat gray, although she appeared to be still in her 30's. It was sort of like a mix of gray and blonde.

"I'm his nephew. Just came to see how he's doing and if he shows any sign of recovery yet…what's your name?"

"Sylvia," she said coming closer to the bed. She raised Al's hand and began taking his pulse. It was at this point that I inquired, "How come his hand is so bad? It appears to be injured or something."

"I heard that it was. He was somewhat delirious and moved his hands about so much that he accidentally struck them against the telephone table next to the bed," she said. "The phone even fell to the floor."

"Hmm, that explains it," I said, now knowing why my aunt and I couldn't reach him on the phone. Thanking her for clearing this up, I then continued, "I see you're a registered nurse," looking at the name tag on her blouse and noticing her last name is Smythe.

"Yes, I'm an RN and have been assigned to care for your uncle since he moved into our ICU—Intensive-Care Unit."

"Appreciate your help Sylvia…but too bad he's not doing so well in recovering."

While driving home I was still thinking about what my pal Charlie McKay told me earlier in the day when we discussed Al's treatment by the doctor at the hospital.

"Frenole, Frenole"—I kept repeating that name to myself as I headed down the busy I-35 freeway loaded with going home traffic. It finally rang a bell. Come to think of it, I did read about a Frankie Frenole a few years ago in the newspaper where Al works. He was a real bummer—linked up with a bunch of drug smugglers and hoods who kept cops busy on the infamous north side of our city. Al, in fact, wrote some newspaper articles about him.

I kept this in mind upon opening the door to my house, but quickly focused on the more enjoyable part of life, namely my pretty wife, Sarah, and our mischievous toddler Matilda, who we often called Maddie for short. Whoever coined the label 'the terrible twos' must have been a busy parent…she was often toddling into some sort of problem, be it pulling on the pup's tail or spilling some hard-to-remove liquid on the carpet. But despite all this, we love her dearly.

I must have still appeared upset when Sarah stopped cooking something for our dinner and asked what's bothering me, and why I was so late. She seemed to have an insight into my very soul at times. This time, I simply passed it off saying, with a grin, "Just my usual rotten day honey…sorry—I was delayed at Al's hospital."

I then kissed her voluptuous lips and while checking over the meal she was ready to dish up, began to share some of what was eating at me from the standpoint of my uncle's condition and my concerns about what was happening to him in that damn hospital.

I was also feeling a bit guilty when I noticed that Sarah stopped eating and tending to.our little daughter. She just sat there with fork in hand, obviously surprised and disappointed by what she was hearing.

Sarah finally uttered, "That's awful, Joe…My God, poor Al. Will he survive? How can we help him?"

Chapter 7

"I don't think we can. It's up to God to pull him out of this. Al obviously was overdosed and hasn't the power to regain consciousness."

"Is he incoherent? Does he show any sign of recognizing you?"

"He doesn't utter a sound, but I'm sure he's in never-never land. That narcotic they have him on must be super-duper. I even felt like putting my ear up to his chest to know if he's breathing."

"Do you know what they have him on? Shouldn't you check further with that doctor?"

"I intend to. I heard that some of it's morphine, but I'm positive he has much more than that in him."

"Are his eyes closed? Does he have any movement at all?"

"Not the slightest. And his eyes are shut and his face ghostly pale. However, I did notice that he has sort of a frightened expression—which I've never seen on my uncle."

Sarah quit asking questions for a while, but after pouring herself some more coffee she inquired: "By the way, what's the name of that doctor you talked to?"

"Frenole—Frenole, Thomas J. Frenole. What's more, I plan to check him out further. Understand he has some shady relatives."

Sarah sat back upon hearing the name. "Gosh, I may know one of those relatives. It's just a guess though. I worked once with Nina Frenole, a real nice gal who told me she has a cousin who's a distinguished doctor in town."

"Geez—I don't know how distinguished he is, but he appears mighty impressed with himself. He didn't give me a clue that he knew what was going on, which is why I plan to question him some more."

"Well, if he's anything like Nina he's very straight and doing his best to bring Al about."

"Time will tell, my dear," I said wiping my face and looking about to see what out little daughter Maddie was up to.

As I reached out to hold her, the phone rang startling me so much that I almost dropped her. I had attached a device on it to amplify the voice of the caller, a clever idea the police taught me a few years back. It mostly turned out to be a loud nuisance, but it sure lets you know you're being summoned.

Still holding Maddie, I was able to reach for the phone—but not before Sarah beat me to it while frowning at my awkward attempts.

I noted that her face paled somewhat by the voice at the other end and she quickly gave the phone to me with a warning: "Joe, it's for you—it's from the hospital and about your uncle."

I was somewhat hesitant to take the phone, after placing Maddie on the floor for fear of what I might be told. I definitely and especially did not want to hear the word "dead."

At first the man's voice on the other end added to the suspense. It was gruff and commanding, as though ready to make a big announcement. And indeed he did.

"Mr. Kavinsky, Joe Kavinsky,?" When I answered, twice that I was indeed him, I was told that I should come to the hospital as soon as possible…that my uncle had taken a turn for the worse.

"Is he dying?" was the only response my trembling voice could utter.

"Not yet. But we're not sure when and if he may be, however. If you can get here quickly—so much the better. The night nurse said you wanted to know if there are any changes, so we're doing that," the voice said, a bit irritated at my hesitation I thought. The caller hung up before I could say thanks…and before I could find out his name.

Upon informing my wife about this latest update on my uncle, she asked, "Do you want me to go with you? I'd like to see Al, too. But don't you think it's about time to call your DEA pal Terry Johnson again since Al's condition is worsening and drug-overdose may be involved?"

"You'd better stay put with Maddie. But yes, I think I'll contact him just in case he has some advice—he's worked with lots of different situations, from the strange to the ridiculous."

When I did call Terry, I could only briefly summarize the situation, letting him know I was summoned to Al's bedside and had to rush there ASAP. I told him I may be needing his help and will call him back again soon.

I was getting to know the way to the hospital quite well, and realized I would probably be pulled over by the highway patrol for speeding if I wasn't driving a squad car that I borrowed for the day. But noting the seriousness of that recent phone call I figured this was indeed an emergency.

I almost ran up the steps to the hospital, and swore a little when I couldn't get the elevator moving fast enough to Al's floor. There must have been ten people getting off at every stop. The doors finally opened allowing me to run to his private room.

But when I did get to the room I was stopped at the entrance by a big guy with a badge in his hand.

"Sorry sir, you can't go in there without proper identification," said the burly fella.

"And who the hell are you?" I inquired. As a cop I was seldom asked for an ID. But I soon realized it was cop against cop, since the guy doing the asking flashed a DEA badge.

"Damn, that Johnson sure acts fast," I muttered.

The guard quickly responded grinning, "Yeah—he sure does. In fact he's in the room right now."

Given the okay to enter—but with a warning that I should be as quiet as possible, I almost tip-toed into the room, which was rather dark in keeping with the setting as my uncle lay motionless. He was being closely observed by not only Johnson but by nurse Sylvia and doctor Frenole.

Hardly anyone looked up as I approached the bed, except for Terry who smiled to recognize my sudden presence. He beckoned me forward and almost whispered in my ear, "Joe, your uncle is extremely overdosed. One of the worst cases I've seen. Glad you called me."

I nodded my thanks that he was here and then, like everyone else, gazed at Al in hope there was some sort of a sign of improvement. But he looked the same as when I saw him last—maybe a little worse. His breathing was much more difficult, I thought...and he still showed no signs of waking up.

Chapter 8

▼

My thoughts were interrupted when the doctor bent over Al and put a stethoscope to his chest. Frowning, he then beckoned Sylvia to his side and after conferring for a few minutes the nurse reached for a strange looking tube.

Although I knew better than to ask what they're doing, I did anyway, and was surprised to hear quite a technical explanation from Terry who's also looking on. "It's done with severe overdosed cases, it's called an intubation, or endotracheal tube—more commonly referred to as an intubate or ET tube. I've seen it used before on guys we've brought in."

Amazed at Terry's medical knowledge, but still not knowing what the hell was going on, I inquired further, "why that?"

"I understand it helps with the breathing and might bring the patient around."

"What if it doesn't?"

"I'm told he can't go on like this much longer, Joe. If this fails he may go into cardiac arrest or, probably worse, he could end up with some brain damage. It's very important that they bring him out of this. I've seen a few cases like this and know what can happen."

"I'd better notify aunt Kay. When do you think they'll know if he can make it?"

"When the doc says so," Terry said with a shrug. With mention of the doctor, I nudged him and whispered, "Let's get out of this room...I want to talk to you away from that doctor."

Without responding, Terry began following me slowly toward the door. Neither doctor nor nurse even noticed our departure. We proceeded past the security guy at the door and once outside, far enough away from the room, sat down on a nearby bench while Terry still looked somewhat puzzled over the reason for such a sudden private discussion.

Still speaking very softly, and continuing to watch the door for anyone wanting to interrupt, I asked my trusty DEA friend, "What do you know about this doctor Frenole?"

"Gosh—nothing at this time. Is there something suspicious about him?"

I then told him what McKay said at the precinct about the possibility of the doctor being related and perhaps even linked in some way with a so-called notorious drug dealer known as Frankie Frenole.

"Sure, I heard of Frankie, but he sort of dropped out of sight years ago. Hell, he caused all kinds of drug problems around the Twin Cities in his days."

"When were those days? I asked. "And would my uncle have been a newspaper man at that time...I'm talking about maybe 30 years or so ago."

"Perhaps, since Al seems to be still in his 60s. But why do you ask?"

"Revenge, Terry, simple revenge. You and I both know that it's mighty dangerous to fool around with the drug mob without paying a price. This may be the price…"

Glancing at his watch, Terry responded "you've got my word, Joe, I'll check into it. But please don't show any signs of being suspicious of anyone around here—we still don't know who's at fault. Only one thing we're sure of now is—to get your uncle out of his nightmare and up again to his typewriter."

"Word processor, Terry," I corrected. "From what I'm told, the typewriter is a thing of the past in the newsroom these days, although my uncle still has one at his house—as well as a computer that assures extra privacy while writing up headline stories."

"It might take some time to really do a reliable job on uncovering what's going on," Johnson said with a shrug, "but we'll keep on top of it—in our most secretive way."

"Yeah, I know. And thanks. I figured you guys are great at sneaking around, but it could be a bit more difficult in a medical institution like this."

"It is more complicated, Joe. Everyone seems to be wearing a gown, and you never know what's going on behind it. In the meantime I think it's safe to call off my bodyguard at the door."

Before returning to Al's room, Terry gave me one more warning, "Also, in the meantime I suggest you try to get a second opinion. Perhaps get one of those Mayo Clinic docs to check him out. Also, doctors seem to know one another quite well…perhaps they'll refer you to a specialist who may be able to give you more of an insight into what's really going on."

"From my experience, Terry, doctors and lawyers are usually in a different league, they often hesitate to talk negatively about one another even when they should," I pointed out.

"Yeah, but what can you loose? Your main concern is to get your uncle well again. Whatever or whoever that takes should be your ultimate goal…right?'

I couldn't disagree with that. I wanted to help as fast as possible. But in my hurry to leave the hospital, I almost forgot I left my coat in Al's room. Almost rushing back to his bedside, I was delayed somewhat by a cleaning lady with red hair and slipped on the floor she was mopping causing me to almost fall…but luckily was supported by a passerby.

As I was heading home with the sad news of my uncle's unconscious struggle to stay alive, my mind began recalling some of the events of the day. Patting my coat to see if anything fell out of it accidentally, especially my wallet, I began wondering who else might have been in and out of that hospital room…and perhaps responsible for Al's condition?

However, I couldn't help but be distracted by the sharp pain in my ankle, twisted from sliding on that floor, nor be a little mad at myself for being so clumsy and that lady with the mop who caused the floor to be so slippery. In fact, I was almost thinking out loud when I began to consider how easy it would be for someone other than a nurse or doctor to get into the room.

Hell, for that matter, even the DEA cop on duty could be fooled into letting someone in pretending to clean the room to keep it safe and spotless for the health of the patient.

I let my imagination roam until parking in my home driveway. Sarah was standing on an outdoor step leading to our house, with Maddie in her arms. I welcomed their smiles and forgot my depression for a brief time on kissing them and even patting my dog Stella who was busy wagging her tail. What a great difference from the gloom and doom I just faced back at that hospital.

"How didja know I was driving up at this time?" I asked Sarah.

"Johnson tipped us off, however he wasn't sure if you would stop off somewhere first."

"Boy, it's good to know so many are looking out for me. I did stop for awhile…I forgot my coat at the hospital, what with all the concern about uncle Al, and had to return for it."

"Do you have anything else to report?" wondered Sarah hoping for better news.

"Nothing much, if anything. He's still barely holding on…without knowing it."

"Did Terry have anything else to say? Any phone numbers to call?"

"Nope. But he did mention he had to leave the hospital, and that his bodyguard would be off duty after 9 tonight."

"What happens then—is he all alone?"

"He didn't say—I presume that he isn't…that there'll be attendants coming in to check on him during the night." I thought about this for a few moments before inquiring "Do you suppose I could stay overnight there, in a nearby room?—you know, just to keep an eye on him."

"You'd have to ask the hospital. I would think they may have an extra bed," replied Sarah, wrinkling her cute little forehead wondering what I had in mind.

"I have this funny feeling—that something or somebody might be after my uncle. If so, I could be close at hand to come to his assistance."

After discussing this further, both Sarah and I felt the best way for me would probably be to just go to the hospital and ask someone in charge where I could stay for the night to be near Al while he's in his coma.

CHAPTER 9
▼

Following a very tasty dinner, which only my darling wife could dish up, I braved the busy freeway again to hopefully talk with a boss or two at the hospital regarding my staying over in one of its empty rooms to keep a check on Al if need be at night. I realized this may be asking a lot since the hospital is considered one of the busiest around the Twin Cities, and usually with a full patient-load. Fortunately, I knew from experience that the bed count may be extremely limited. There were many times I had to be there to talk to those either injured by some violent crime…or criminals themselves who were shot, stabbed or drugged—but willing to talk to cops.

Whatever the case, however, I was determined to protect Al and be there for him, as he has always been for me since I was little boy. I learned how to swing a bat at T-ball, run around bases, and even shoot baskets and kick soccer balls with help of his coaching, in the absence of my own dad who died young in a car accident.

Strange as it seemed, I was directed once again to Sylvia, the blonde and premature gray hair nurse who was on duty in Al's room the last time we met. She seemed quite surprised by my request to be near my uncle during the night. At first she said there were no vacant rooms available, but a passing nurse overhearing us said a special visitor room had just opened and may be able to accommodate me. Fortunately I brought an intercom system and secretly installed and hid it in Al's room and mine when no one was looking. I also took out a pillow and blanket from my brief case and made a makeshift bed. Before lying down I noticed Sylvia walking away, sort of upset over my success in finding a cozy little bedroom close to my uncle's.

It didn't take me long to dose off, after watching some boring TV programs, and I slept soundly for what seemed to be a few hours. But as I shifted over on my back and heard myself snoring, I thought I also heard some sound coming from Al's room. I snorted a little, closed my mouth to stop snoring, then propped myself up on a pillow to make sure I could hear better.

Sure enough, there was something going on in the room next to me. It was almost a mumbling sound over my intercom set, but it definitely was something. I checked the clock near my bed and found it was only 4 a.m., so what the hell could be going on at this ungodly hour?

Pushing off my blanket, I didn't even look for my slippers as I dashed from my room in my tattered old pajamas and made a beeline toward my uncle's room.

It was mostly dark, except for a dim light at his bedside. I could barely make out the small figure hovering over his bed. It was a woman's figure. She was peering down at Al, although the darkness nearly prevented her from seeing him.

Al was still motionless and apparently unconscious. But despite this, the mysterious woman kept mumbling over his bed as if he could communicate with her.

Fortunately, I had a flashlight. There was no need to search for a light switch, and when I focused the light on the unknown room guest, the suddenness of going from extreme darkness to brightness startled both of us and was quite revealing.

She wore a veil on her head. Not a Muslim type scarf...but the type I remember as a boy that some women wore in Catholic churches, a custom very seldom seen these days. She also held what appeared to be a string of beads and some cards.

"Who are you? And why are you in the dark with my uncle?" I demanded. She appeared to be as surprised as I am. "You're not supposed to be here, didn't someone tell you? There was a guard at this door. What are you doing here?"

"Please, my name is Marlis and I'm a health-care advocate assigned to this hospital. I work at night when the need arises. I was told that this man was in dire need for some prayers at his bedside in hope he can, by the grace of God, be restored to health."

"What's a health-care advocate anyway?"

"We help those on the brink of death and prepare them and their loved ones to cope when and if it comes. We also take an active role in an effort to enhance a patient's medical treatment."

With that, I lowered my flashlight and found the light switch. She was pleased to get the glaring flash light from her eyes. I asked further, "But how can you enhance his treatment?"

"Mostly by prayers, sir, but also by medical observation. If I sense anything wrong, I notify the proper medical authorities immediately. I've studied a lot about drug victims."

My thoughts regarding her comments were suddenly distracted by the intrusion of the cleaning lady who wondered if the room needed any more of her attention. I figured it strange she should be concerned about this so late, but at this point I was feeling ready for more sleep.

Upon given the okay by the health advocate to enter, the woman with the mop began using it around the floor, and that's when I decided to depart for bed. However, on my way out I couldn't help but again notice the very red hair of the cleaning lady.

After a restless night on the hard hospital bed, I looked into my uncle's room to see that he's still breathing, downed a quick cup of coffee in the hospital diner, and headed out to my precinct to see what else awaits me. However, I no sooner got to my desk when I received an urgent phone call that I was needed on Hennepin Avenue in downtown Minneapolis to check out a fatal shooting.

Finding a squad car in the precinct garage was no easy matter. When I did, I raced out on the busy streets, turned on my siren and headed to the crime scene ready for God knows what, realizing on Hennepin this could range anywhere from a strangling to a drive-by shooting. As usual, the first person to look for is the street cop who came upon the scene first. He gave me some background, stating that the victim reportedly was from a rival gang who resisted turning over some drugs. A bullet through the head was the result. After checking the body—a young guy not even in his twenties—I wrote down the grim details and tucked them into my pocket after also getting as much information as possible from those who may have witnessed the crime.

Chapter 10

Before getting back into my squad, I noticed the large dome of the cathedral nearby. With uncle Al's condition still in my mind as well as the body of a young guy killed in cold blood, I figured it might be wise to visit this church and try to figure things out a little with the Almighty. I realized even the best of detectives couldn't always piece together some of the insane and horrible happenings they encounter without some divine guidance.

Going into the church, also gave me a feeling of humility. In fact, after removing my hat I proceeded down to the front pew. Praying for help seemed easy, inspired by the many statues of saints and, of course, Jesus looking down on me from the altar. After some brief prayers and meditation, especially for my uncle, I once more entered the real world, getting into my squad and taking off for my cluttered desk at the precinct where so many calls for help are posted.

It wasn't until I returned home that evening when I could really relax and think about how lucky I am to have such a lovely wife and child, as well as Stella the pup of course. Following dinner, we all sat around and enjoyed our blessings, even though the pup did an accident on the carpet and Maddie began screaming when told it was bedtime.

Sarah and I also hit the sack only a few hours later. But we both seemed very restless. No time for love making. I couldn't get the body of that slain young man from my mind, and, of course, how my uncle Al was doing. Was he getting out of his coma by now? And would I be notified of any change in his condition at night?

I almost bumped into Sarah while turning and tossing in bed. She was still awake, however, and also must have been thinking of Al. The first thing she asked was "Joe, it's been bothering me—what thoughts do you believe are in a comatose person's mind?"

Having been around overdosed victims, including criminals in emergency rooms, drug addicts, and even God fearing victims in a vegetative state, I recall a few who survived and who related some of their thoughts to me while they were 'out of this world.'

"I remember some saying it's like being back home with friends...many who passed away years ago. A Catholic nun I know and greatly respect who was in a long coma after a car accident told me she thought she was back in the convent again meeting some old nuns she knew from years ago. She was telling them about poor students and wondering what she can do to help them. She said she felt alive and young again and never felt pain or thoughts of the accident. Others described it as an out-of-body experience. It's often referred to as 'crossing over.' Some even mumble while in bed as though talking to someone they apparently see. Others say it's like falling in a tunnel until noticing a bright light at the bottom."

With that, Sarah snuggled closer to me, saying: "Joe, what do you suppose is at the bottom of that tunnel, and why the light?" I could only reply, when you get to the light I understand you're dead, you meet God almighty. Suppose it's just part of that 'crossing over.'
Kinda scary, though...isn't it?"
"Oh Joe, your poor uncle. You must help bring him out of this as quickly as possible."

"But how?—I've already checked into numerous ways, met with doctor and nurses, and kept the DEA closely informed."

"How about going to our famous clinic in Rochester for medical advice?"

"Good idea, but I really should check with the DEA first. I don't want to interfere with what they may be doing. However, I do want to inform Terry about some of the people I met recently who might be considered suspects."

Before leaving for my precinct in the morning, and after swallowing enough black coffee to make sure I wouldn't fall asleep at my desk due to my almost sleepless night at home, I kept thinking about the highly respected Mayo clinic only about 70 miles south of my house. I guess I really should get a second opinion from one of those distinguished doctors down there who should know the latest treatment, if there is any, to wake a patient from such a deep coma.

With the thought that this could be part of my conversation with Johnson, as well as that list I compiled about possible suspects, I glanced at the kitchen clock and figured I had enough time to get in a quick call to Terry before dashing off to work. I lucked out, it was as though he had been waiting to hear from me. My opening conversation focused on the growing list of people in my mind who have been acting rather suspiciously around Al.

I was careful to note such characters as Marlis the hooded health care advocate who in the dead of night was checking him out, the somewhat mysterious nurse Sylvia, doctor Frenole and, just in case it mattered—even the cleaning lady.

I gave him as much description and other information I had on each one, unfortunately it was all rather sketchy. But hell, these DEA sleuths should be able to take it from here and uncover enough about each one to see if they actually do measure up as a suspect.

And I could provide first names…except for the cleaning lady who I just got a glimpse of as she was entering the hospital room on my way out.

"About all I can remember is that she has the reddest hair I've ever seen. She could be in her late 30s and slightly over five feet tall. She also was a little overweight, too, as I recall."

I was somewhat surprised that Terry seemed a little perturbed. "Damn it, Joe, you're supposed to be a great detective and our undercover—why the hell couldn't you get a better fix on her…last names would help, too."

I hesitated, knowing that my only defense was saying: "Now remember this was very late at night and I was nearly falling asleep. But I'm sure the hospital office could let you know.
I'm running very fast these days trying to save Al. Hopefully they don't have too many red heads among their cleaning crews."
Terry accepted this excuse, without chewing me out further, and once again in his usual cheerful way said he will quickly get back to me regarding what the DEA finds out about those on my suspect list, as vague as this might be.

Sighing a little, momentarily comforted by this, I nearly forgot to mention my plan to contact the Rochester clinic for a special doctor who may be noted for bringing overdosed victims back to reality. But fortunately I was able to bring this up before Johnson clicked off.

I must have sounded like a beggar asking for his permission when I presented the reasons for getting in touch with such a doctor—if indeed one is available. But I was surprised how quickly he responded.

"Hell yes! As I indicated before I think that's a super idea. It sure wouldn't conflict with what we're doing. As I recall, you knew some of the docs down there when you were trying to catch up with those drug lords at the clinic who were on their way to our giant mall—didn't you?"

"Yeah, and some knew Al. I remember he was talking to the clinic's public relations director to obtain the names of those at the clinic tied in with the terrorist attempts at entering the Upper Midwest by posing as patients from the Mideast.

"Do you remember the PR guy's name?"

"Matter of fact, I do. It's Sam…Sam Stone. If anyone would know who the best doc would be, it'd be Stone. Besides, he owes my uncle a debt. Al wrote a great article on that medical clinic in his newspaper, even though he used the unwitting public relations man as a way to find the clinic's medical staff who may be tied in with the terrorists visiting the clinic."

"Go for it, Joe! He's your opener. This along with our surveillance teams should help discover what's happening to Al. In fact, we're going to try more than that. We plan to not only have cameras hidden in Al's room to catch any suspicious visitors—but also mirrors."

Frankly, the mirror bit threw me, at first I thought what the hell would anyone be doing looking in a mirror. Of course, some may be egotistical maniacs. It all made sense, however, when he continued to explain.

"Joe, have you ever noticed when you place the tip of your finger against a regular mirror you can see the tip. If you can't—this may be a 2-way mirror. With these special mirrors our guys will be able to see everything in the whole damn room and then some. Sort of like the 2-way glass walls used during the interrogation of suspects used at your police lineups."

"Won't they get a bit suspicious about all this?"

"Not really they'll be in appropriate places and small enough not to be noticed. They'll look like just part of the furniture. These, plus our surveillance cameras, should do the trick."

I couldn't argue with this, knowing that the DEA's full of so-called tricks. It wasn't until the next day when I heard from Johnson, only this time he once again seemed irritated.

My first thought was…what the hell did I goof up now?

"Guess what?-There ain't no red-head cleaner!" were the first words out of his mouth, as ungrammatical as they sounded.

For a moment, I thought my DEA buddy flipped. Was he looking to clean his hair?—but it wasn't red, it was more brown and slightly wavy like mine. I like to kid him at times by saying his is also wavy—waving goodbye. But I couldn't see if he had his silly grin on his face.

But he was in no way ready for anything other than being serious. "We've checked into all those characters you gave us and already have somewhat of a reading on them except for that cleaning lady. The hospital just doesn't have anyone mopping up rooms with that color of hair."

Despite all this, Terry once again pledged to continue looking at the comings and goings in Al's room and would check back with me later to give a final report on the possible suspect list…especially if anything of importance shows up on the cameras—and of course in the mirrors.

After a tiring and depressive day dealing with the depravity of humanity I often encounter in my work, I was eager to get home with my consoling wife and mischievous toddler and dog.

However, it wasn't always easy to get home, thanks to the Twin Cities' gosh awful spring highway construction work. It was almost bumper-to-bumper now, and I could see why the police have so many calls regarding driver-rage, especially at this time of year.

But it did give me more time to think back on what both Terry and my wife said about checking with the clinic experts for a 'second opinion' on how to bring Al out of his dreamland.

When I finally did reach home, I shoved dinner in the background in hope of first trying to contact the clinic PR guy Stone. From what I heard from Al regarding public relations folks, they often work late so there may be a good chance at contacting him before he's also off to the serenity of his home.

Considering the entanglements one can run into just trying to make an appointment at this busy clinic, I was quite lucky to get a human voice on my first attempt at asking for Stone. The receptionist, to my surprise, said she believed he was still in his office and she'd contact him immediately. Although he seemed rather hurried, he took time to listen to me about Al and was very cordial as I suspect most PR guys are taught to be.

He seemed to be very sympathetic and willing to help, mentioning once again how helpful Al was in getting that "excellent" story on the clinic in the Sunday issue of the Star. My ploy was working—without any dispute about a followup story that also appeared on the clinic in a later issue regarding the long wait sometimes involved with patient registrations.

But there was hesitation for a few moments that had me worried when I asked what doctor he could suggest to be contacted who is especially known for his work with comatose patients. Noting that the clinic has many excellent docs specializing in this, he kept me on hold for what seemed like many minutes before getting back to me.

"Mr. Kavinsky, I've checked this out. Having worked closely with our medical staff I can safely say that perhaps the best and most experienced in such a case would be doctor Hamid Lahn. He's also a very distinguished

MD and researcher in this field and teaches our residents about this type of condition. Indeed, he has authored many articles on its treatment which have appeared in leading medical journals around the nation."

This sounded good enough for me, and brought me to the next question: "How can I reach this doctor Lahn?"

"I'll have him call you. Like me, he usually works late and perhaps may even try to reach you later today or early tomorrow. As you know, I'm sure, I really like Al and respect him as a journalist. I'm so sorry to hear about his condition. Please keep me posted on his health."

Assuring him that I would, I returned once more to the now somewhat cold meal Sarah had served up, but couldn't resist discreetly giving a few scraps to the begging pup sitting up—causing Maddie to giggle and Sarah to frown.

Chapter 11

▼

After dinner I couldn't help but keep an eye on my watch in hope that doctor Lahn may be calling. I knew it was a long shot, however, so I also decided to briefly take a few moments in the meantime to talk to Terry to recap my conversations with Sam Stone. By now, I memorized his special cell phone number and the 'alias' I had to use in my contacts with that supposedly clever DEA agent…"JOKE" which lets him know who's calling. He came up with this since he said JO relates to my first name and KE to Kavinsky. Don't know where he got the E, however.

Thinking of rather strange names, I made it a point to tell Terry when he answered that the doc's first name is Hamid, which sounds more like it belongs to one of those so-called terrorists from the Mideast. Of course, I realized I was running nervous having personally observed so much drug terrorism and the like.

"You can't tell anything about just a name," he calmly assured me. "I'd strongly recommend you take him up on this. Keep your eyes on him, though, and we'll certainly do likewise."

"Why do you think this is all happening to poor uncle Al?"

"Who knows? As you said it could be 'pay back' time. You and I both know how Al used to focus on those damn drug kingpins in his articles. This may be their way of stopping him. Or then again, it may be someone we least suspect. Someone who's a real role model and highly respected among his peers and community. In any case, we'll call you when we find out more with our sophisticated spying devices."

Given this official go-ahead, I proceeded at once to get in touch with doctor Lahn. Again, I thought it would take forever to contact a busy clinic doc, but no sooner had I lit another cigarette to prepare for a long delay than Lahn returned my call.

I quickly introduced myself and smoothed the way to conversing with this busy clinician by noting that I was referred to him by the clinic's director of public relations and communications. He quickly responded, in a very gentle tone, that he was informed about the circumstances of my call by Sam and that he was ready to phone me if I hadn't called soon because of the emergency of the situation.

I noticed there was no trace of any Mideast accent and felt comfortable speaking with him like I would a native Minnesotan—except unlike the way we talk up here there were no 'yeps' or 'you betchas' in his vocabulary.

Knowing he already knew some of the background about my uncle's condition, but trying to be sure that the necessary secrecy, privacy and caution takes place, I suggested we talk further about this when he drives up to see Al at a small and almost secluded café near the hospital called Smitty's. But he interrupted me immediately by saying, "No Mr. Kavinsky—I think we have to act faster than that—considering your uncle's predicament."

He added, "I come to the Twin Cities quite often. But since I do have other matters to check out, I cannot tell you exactly when I'll arrive, however. It may even be in the evening or early morning when you may not be available like I am to see your uncle. But I most certainly will get back to you promptly regarding my findings. You can count on that."

Since he had all the information needed to quickly contact me and had assured me there would be no trouble in visiting Al because of his special credentials, I had no problem with this. Also, knowing that Terry has his surveillance and tricky mirror system always "turned on", I shrugged off any doubts that this doctor would go unnoticed in Al's room no matter when he arrives.

After another restless night, which probably also kept my wife from sleeping well, I gulped down a fast breakfast, almost emptied the coffee pot, and was all set to dash out the door after kissing Sarah and my child goodbye. Sarah sensed my anxiety, knowing I was in a hurry to hear from doctor Lahn, which was why my kiss was more like a peck compared to the usual long and sexy smooches I loved to give her heading out to work.

But before I could put my keys in my car's ignition I heard Sarah calling me back. "Joe, it's the clinic doctor…he wants to talk to you right away." I don't even remember closing the car door in my great rush to get to the phone, still being held by my wife at the doorway. She was smiling over being able to catch me before I reached the fast freeways.

"Mr. Kavinsky, your uncle has had too much sedation. I administered a drug called Narcan for overdosed patients and notified hospital attendants to fix his oxygen device to prevent the morphine being pumped into him from going out of control and affecting his oxygen supply."

I wondered why the hell this wasn't done earlier with all the attendants in and out of his room? He let me know without asking. "That machine usually makes a loud noise to notify everyone nearby that it isn't working right, but in this case it must have been accidentally disconnected and unable to beep."

"Who do we blame for that?"

"Don't know. But it certainly wasn't the nurses since they aren't authorized to be tampering with any of the connections."

He explained further, "When this happens the patient doesn't breathe deep enough and the machine, called a pulse oximeter, is supposed to beep because the oxygen level gets too low.
Narcotic affects the breathing center. Some patients are more sensitve to this than others. In the case of your uncle, it's amazing that he's still holding on."

"Has his brain been affected?"

"I'll have to consult with other specialists, hopefully today—and also with his surgeon."
He continued, "But he needs much more treatment to snap out of this. Of course, I also need permission to carry this out from his family or others close to him who may know about his health care directives. For example does he have a document showing what he wishes in case of life-threatening emergencies? like being kept alive or not in such situations?"

"What the heck is that?"

"It's the legal paper needed telling the doctor the patient's will to live."

"I'll have to ask his wife to obtain this. How soon do you need it?"

"The sooner the better, for your uncle's sake."

I felt like okaying this right now, but also knew I had to make sure Terry wanted to proceed with this after getting more information on the doctor from the security gadgets he had installed. I knew aunt Kay would be eager to go ahead with whatever would help Al.

Not knowing if Terry or my aunt would be on hand to take my phone call, I told Lahn it might take some time to get the approvals. He sounded disappointed and reminded me I should let him know as soon as possible to avoid Al being brain damaged. Rather than try explaining this to aunt Kay, who often gets confused over details, I called Johnson first and was lucky again to catch him at his office. But he said to wait a bit longer until all reports on Lahn were studied. The camera and mirror input, for instance, were still being processed, as well as other input.

Although disturbed by delays, I was comforted somewhat by knowing Terry was so concerned about Al as to want to double-check everything involving his care-givers while knowing the urgency needed to help him. I clicked off after thanking him for the update, but reminded him again that I'm anxiously looking forward to letting Lahn go ahead with his help.

My next phone conversation also shook me up somewhat. It came shortly after I grabbed some more coffee from the nearby machine and finally began checking out my investigative projects for the day. The call was from Al's city editor, Fred Hanson, who my uncle liked and respected. Al always said Fred knows a good story when it shows up and is always looking for a news break, regardless of the controversy and consequences. But I figured this call was probably just to find out how Al was getting along. It was to begin with…but not for long.

"Joe, what the hell's happening to Al?" were the first words out of Fred's mouth. "I've tried to call his room and no one answers. How's he doing? He told me he was going in for a simple rotator cuff operation but no one in the newsroom has heard from him since."

Once I updated him, he seemed so surprised he began stammering. "But…but Al thought he'd be just in and out of that darn hospital. He told me he'd be back at work in a few days. I knew he wanted to cause he's been so involved with a story he's been preparing. It's about half finished and still on his desk. We've been anxious to see the completed version, too, of course. It would be another scoop for your uncle who always seems to be 'in on the know'. We're all heart sick over this and will appreciate being kept informed whenever you can let us know."

My curiosity got the better of me. "Fred—hold the phone! What you said about the story he's been working on—what and who's involved? I know my uncle's been keeping to himself lately and has been quite silent about what he's been doing. Usually, as you know, he's always the first to socialize and chatter."

"Yeah, I know. He's been that way lately since coming across a story again dealing with drugs. But, Joe, he sort of swore me not to say anything about it to anyone. I agreed, realizing that it may be one of the biggest stories of the year for our newspaper."

There was a pause, as both Fred and I both wondered if now is the time to talk about this.

Fred broke the brief silence with "What the hell, you're his nephew and a cop to be admired. Your uncle is so damn proud of you. I sure don't want this to get around before we finish the story, Joe. But here's what I know at this point:

"Al was tipped off by one of his many sources that a big politician in town is into drugs and drug smuggling. That politician is so powerful he could probably fire me, you and your police chief. But he's a son-of-a-bitch and Al has the goods on him. But please don't say anything about this yet…since we still have to confirm some of our findings. That's what Al was doing these past few weeks when he wasn't writing about this at his word processor."

I sat back and lit another cigarette, inhaled deeply and blew out the smoke as I thought over what the editor was saying, I wasn't too surprised. Al could dig out the toughest stories.

I also realized Fred was taking a chance telling me about this. However, I felt he may have done so purposely knowing I'm a detective. But my being an undercover for the DEA was unknown to nearly everyone—and Al was determined to keep this a secret from all his associates in the press. But how much he talked about me to his fellow news staffers was kind of unknown.

"So who is this politician, do I know him?" I asked.

"I'm sure you do. But I'd rather not say on the phone. Let's meet somewhere private so I can get into this a little more without anyone else knowing."

"What about the Hilltop for lunch today? It's off beat and far enough from the city, yet still somewhat convenient for both of us," I suggested.

"I know where it's at...and I'll bring Al's incomplete manuscript with me," he said.

Settling on noon, I still had enough time to check into the shooting of that young guy near the church I was visiting. I talked some more with the cops who were at the site but the most I could obtain before heading out to the Hilltop was that he had been mixed up with cocaine dealers for some time and had squealed on some of the competitive gang members who put a contract out on him. I also was able to talk a little with his mother for more information, which was so sad that it further depressed me, but took my mind off of constantly wondering about Al and how he was doing.

However, it wasn't long before I began thinking about Al again as well as what his editor was telling me. The thought also came to mind that I should update Terry on this, which led me to stopping at a donut shop enroute back to work. It was where my uncle and I used to meet at times when we had some quiet time. Being somewhat acquainted with this little joint I knew exactly where to sit and dial Johnson. It was ideal for talking on a tiny cell phone. There was hardly any noise, only occasional creaking of the nearby door as customers came and left.

Only this time, my luck ran out with contacting Terry. He left a voice message telling callers he would be gone until mid afternoon. I left a message in return, noting that I'll try calling him again later in the day and that it was important that we talk. In a way, the more I thought about it, having some extra time was okay since I certainly didn't want to go into much detail with anyone on the subject now until meeting with the editor.

When I got up to leave, I spotted Sylvia the nurse. She also saw me. I wondered why she would be so far from the hospital, the donuts weren't that good in this place. She came by my table but didn't smile. Wanting to know the latest about Al, I made it a point to inquire. She treated me rather coldly, however, and said she'd been off duty from the hospital for a few days. When she left, I noticed she got into an expensive looking car, like a Mercedes, driven by someone with his coat collar up so high I couldn't see his face. Scratching my head over what seemed out of the ordinary for a working girl I saw them drive off as though in a hurry. I didn't have much time to wonder about this, however, looking at my watch I realized I had to rush off to see the editor. As I sped along I kept wondering who the heck that crooked politician could be.

Driving to the Hilltop was always a challenge, with its winding roads and sharp curves. But, as I told the editor, this made it all the more private for a serious conversation. I never met Fred, but could tell the moment I arrived that he was the one at the table in a corner of the restaurant with a pencil behind his ear reading a newspaper. He looked all ready to go to press.

He also recognized me immediately, noting I looked exactly like my uncle described me to some of his fellow 'wordsmiths' around the newsroom, even though he didn't notice the revolver and badge under my coat.

With that introduction, he tried getting right into the purpose of our meeting.

He first looked about making sure he couldn't be heard by passersby, which further added to the suspense. But to lighten up the situation, and before he could begin, I motioned to the passing waitress to take our orders so we wouldn't be interrupted. After that, Fred leaned over to me and said softly, "Joe, your uncle did an excellent job in finding out what was going on behind the scenes involving one of our leading city councilmen."

"And what was that—and who was it?"

"Drugs and lots of it. The 'who', according to Al's report, is none other than John Elroy."

I guess I looked so surprised that he quickly added, "That's right, the clean cut, honorable young councilman who's now running for mayor."

"Is Al sure? A story like this could be explosive to Elroy's career," I noted.

"Dynamite! But every bit of information regarding this was jotted down in Al's notes which he was using to write this exclusive article. Unfortunately, he couldn't complete it because of this damn operation."

He showed me some of the notes, convincing me that Al was on the right track When I asked for a copy, he refused politely saying that when my uncle departed his office for the hospital he made the editor promise not to release it yet.

"Do you suppose Elroy knew Al was working on this?"

"I don't know how he could, but I'm sure you know how word gets out among the criminal element. Also, our newspaper has to make damn sure everything is accurate or we could be in for an enormous law suit."

Wiping some sweat from my forehead, I wondered, hopefully, about any possible extra ways to help get the goods on Elroy. My first thought, of course, was contacting the DEA through Johnson. I didn't mention this, however, since I wanted to leave the editor with a promise not to tell anyone until all of Al's input is confirmed. But who would be more credible in confirming this than Terry? I'm sure he could already have some knowledge about all this, knowing how he pokes his nose into anything smelling a little suspicious, especially drugs.

Chapter 12

After we left the Hilltop, along with a bigger than usual tip for the waiter for not being interrupted, Fred and I went our separate ways...the wiser for our meeting, of course. I didn't wait until arriving at the precinct, however, to call Terry since I was going by the donut shop again and knew this would be a good time and place to phone him.

My first words were "Terry—do you know a John Elroy?"

After a long pause, I heard, "Yeah, but I'd never vote for him."

"I wouldn't either, judging from what I've heard about him," I responded.

"Whatever you've heard, it isn't enough...but tell me about it," he urged.

Recapping my conversation with Al's boss, Terry listened intently before saying:
"Yes, he certainly isn't the prince portrayed by his fellow political supporters. However I didn't know anyone knew of this besides the DEA—it's considered topnotch secret, or as our homeland security would put it...a real red alert. Al apparently was really sitting on something red hot,

he had quite a scoop since Elroy seems to be deep into drug dealing. He appears to be in cahoots with the local druglords. Where your uncle got his information, though, is quite a mystery considering our sources have had one hell of a time trying to get something on this kingpin."

Terry added, "We still haven't enough to pin him down. But from what you're telling me, Al has notes that could dethrone his kingdom."

This made me gulp a little. "Do you think this has something to do with Al's overdose?"

I thought at first we had a bad connection since it took so long for Terry to respond, but I knew I had just recharged my cell phone battery recently.

"Good question…yeah, it could have something, or even everything to do with that. Who knows someone may be out to stop that story. Al's been writing so many stories about drug dealing and the like that it could be both *halt and pay back* time."

"What do we do further—God, my uncle is still desperate for help. We can't just let this go on and on this way."

"Just calm down!—help is on the way. Evidence is forthcoming, and we should be able to come to the rescue very, very soon." Knowing that *soon* may not be fast enough, I could only hope that it meant giving Dr. Lahn the go-ahead to begin his treatment of Al. I was sure by this time aunt Kay was wearing out her rosary praying for him. I tried praying too, whenever I could, but my work with other victims needing help was a big distraction. The mother of that young lad gunned down, for instance, was also very much on my mind, as I checked the long list of gangs around the area who might resort to fatal payback violence on anyone betraying them.

I no sooner re-opened the files on the drug killing of this guy when I got a call from Johnson again. He seemed almost out of breath this time and spoke very fast.

"Joe, I know you're busy, but I gotta tell you this right away. We received our pictures back of visitors to your uncle's room and I must say they're darn interesting-surprisingly so."

I felt my gut tightening from anticipation. But I sure hoped to hell that it wouldn't mean I have to call off doctor Lahn's help. Terry wasn't too positive about this, however.

"Lahn may be okay, but frankly we were amazed about his visit. Our cameras showed that he spent only a brief time looking at your uncle. What interested us most, however, was his intimacy with the night nurse."

"Wow—slow up. What kind of intimacy? I didn't even know he knew her."

"Well apparently he does, and very well."

"What do you mean by that?"

"Our two-way mirror caught them in the dressing room kissing."

"He was making out in the dressing room?" I almost hollered.

"Don't jump to conclusions, Joe. It was more affectionate than passionate. However, I'm not sure, they may indeed be lovers."

"But my God, he's old enough to be her father."

"And who knows…he may be."

"What do you mean?...I was only kidding when I said that."

"Well, I'm not. We have to check into this further...what we know so far is that Lahn is indeed a skilled physician regarding the recovery of overdosed victims. Who knows, he may be just flirting, or perhaps Sylvia was a medical student of his and he fell for her. You must admit, she's quite a looker, despite her strange two-tone hair."

"Terry this is no time to be funny. If he's good, then let him help Al. I don't care what Lahn does in his private life."

"Agreed, nor do we care...unless it isn't lawful. We just want to do a little more research on him Joe and we guarantee you'll be more at ease."

"Can you guarantee when? I'm sure Al would like to know, too. After all, he's been in 'la-la land' long enough."

"Yes—but give us another day or so. In the meantime don't do anything to make him suspicious, nor Sylvia. They still may be your best, and-God forbid, the last hope in reviving him. In the meantime, we'll also keep our eyes on Elroy to see that he doesn't get in the way."

Needless to say, the rest of my day was anything but restful. Although I was getting used to suspense, I felt like I was walking on a very short and narrow plank above very turbulent waters. Frankly, I wasn't sure which way to go first, realizing I still hadn't officially obtained aunt Kay's okay for Al to receive special treatment from doctor Lahn—or Al's health care directive stating his wishes—as in the case of those wishing to be kept on life support or dying.

Thank God I was able to sit down with my aunt in her peaceful home and explain the situation as calmly as possible. Surprisingly, she took it rather calmly. Matter of fact, she and Al had recently prepared health care directives at the suggestion of their financial advisor. And yes, Al didn't want to linger on should he be in a life-and-death situation involving long-time emergency care, especially if it wasn't likely to help. As the saying goes: "Pull the Plug." But the thought of this didn't console her much. Her dainty little hanky was getting very wet as she dabbed at her eyes and I could sense I had better quickly obtain both the directive and the note she wrote as his wife authorizing continued treatment if this meant more possible success than failure. With these in hand, I kissed her goodbye and left before I also started to cry.

To take a break from all this sorrow, I stopped at my home enroute to my busy detective work and recapped my aunt Kay's hospital visit to my wife…who's always been a good listener.

Chapter 13

Sarah also agreed that it probably was best to let Lahn do his thing…although agreeing it was a bit weird to find him smooching the nurse behind closed doors. I felt relieved from this "grind of crime" I encounter so often and, even though rushed to capture some bad guys, I took some relaxing time out to play with Maddie and chase after the pup with a toy in his mouth.

But best of all, I got in some extra loving with my voluptuous wife. She gave me the much needed energy to get back to work with a smile on my face.

When I arrived at my desk, however, the smile soon vanished. Liz my secretary had another Post-it note stuck on the glass wall of my bailiwick. It had a scribbled message notifying me to call the cell phone number of Johnson, with the words Important and Urgent underlined. But as I reached for the phone I was stopped by the cold stare of Chief Hermes. He was standing at the door of his office looking at me sternly with his arms crossed. I quickly knew why when he sauntered over to see me…he was wondering why the hell I was gone so often from my work which seemed to be piling up on my desk.

He especially wanted to know how I was progressing with the investigation of that young druggie found murdered near downtown. Stalling somewhat to recall that case, I quietly related the brief facts I collected and then asked to be taken off that assignment due to my uncle's worsening condition and my frequent need to help him. He accepted this, even asking if one of his cops should again be guarding Al's room. I declined, since this may get in the way-more than help.

Reducing my workload, I again reminded my secretary not to stick Post-It notes for me where passersby can see them. She apologized once more and then remembered I also had an extra one she didn't show me since she didn't want to interrupt my talking with the chief.

It was from doctor Lahn. Although I now had most of the information he needed authorizing him to proceed, I remembered Terry wanted another day to be sure this guy should be involved with Al. That's why I lied a little, telling him I still had some problems rounding up all the authorization he requested. I emphasized, however, that I should be able to give him the go-ahead within the next 24 hours or so. I had my fingers crossed, knowing that I was buying time and only hoping that Terry would be getting back to me by that time with an overall good report on Lahn.

Before clicking off, I was almost tempted to ask Lahn if he knew the night nurse. But I realized this might make him suspicious and who knows what could happen. I certainly didn't want to do anything that might be harmful to Al.

Lighting a cigarette while glancing at all the paperwork on my desk, I focused again on reducing it somewhat even though the chief gave me a break from much of it. I sincerely wanted to dig into the shooting on Hennepin more and called the forensic lab to see if they had come up with anything that could be helpful. They said the bullet was from an ordinary

.38. However, the body was loaded with narcotics, including even GBL, a so called "rape party drug."

The lab findings definitely indicated that this was a young-person crime and revenge of some kind. Hell, just about any teenager could get some of this, as well as the gun considering the state's permission of concealed weapons and the like.

Before I could proceed any further, my phone rang again. I sort of hesitated, hoping to get further into this shooting case, but when noticing it was from Johnson I grabbed it wondering if he had some more news for me regarding Lahn.

"Forget Lahn for a minute, let's talk first about Elroy," were Terry's opening words.

For God's sake, has he forgotten time is running out fast for my uncle? I kept thinking…

"Joe, we've learned that Elroy seems to be the new king of drug lords around town. But what's more alarming is he's connected closely with Frankie Frenole."

So far there was nothing very alarming about this, until I heard the next report.

"And do you know who our mysterious redhead cleaning lady is connected to?…none other than Frankie. In fact, our master sleuths here have found that her real last name is Frenole. Whether she's a sister, daughter or shirt-tail cousin of Frankie's is still unsure. What this adds up to, though, is that we should keep her the hell out of Al's room."

"But how do we do that without arousing lots of suspicion?"

"You mean how do *you* do it…we can keep our guard at the door but then they'll all wonder if we're on to them. As part of his family, if you ask the hospital to avoid having your uncle's room cleaned since it seems to bother him more, they should be able to stop it, at least for a while…hopefully until we can positively prove that cleaning gal is doing something to Al. Our cameras haven't come up with anything yet."

"So what do I do in the meantime? My uncle may be long gone before all this is proven. Seems to me we're getting more concerned about catching someone than trying to help someone clinging to life."

"Which brings up my next important point. The DEA has not found anything wrong with doctor Lahn. We checked and double-checked his resume and everything we could get our hands on to learn more about him. You're right, he is in from the Mideast, but in no way have we come up with anything evil about him. According to our researchers, he's never been charged with any mal-practice and has an outstanding record of medical accomplishments."

"In other words, I can let him help Al without worrying about it."

"It's your call, Joe. I'm only saying what we've found out. Accidents can happen, of course, like a slip of a knife. But if I were you I'd lose no more time in proceeding with him."

With that in mind, my next phone conversation was with doctor Lahn. I could reach him quickly by cell phone…he had my number and I had his. He must have been waiting for my call on his monitor since it seemed he immediately answered by saying in a very somber tone, "Hello Mr. Kavinsky, I've been expecting to hear from you sooner than this. Your uncle needs help right now or we'll be losing him."

I answered rather frightfully, "Go ahead—do what is necessary. We have all the documents and permissions requested for what you want to do for him. Just do it as fast as possible *please!*."

"I'm on the way to do that now. I'll be helped by a nurse, of course."

"You mean the night nurse?"

"Yes, she's already on duty."

I couldn't hold back with that opening, and before he could click off asked as casually as possible, "Do you know her well?"

"Yes, very well and I regard her quite highly…a very good nurse and, I might add, a very good niece."

I hope he didn't hear me sighing in relief. An uncle kissing his niece certainly isn't a crime.

"I haven't seen Sylvia in a long time and was completely surprised to find her in the hospital hallway making her rounds. In fact, I understand she works the wing that your uncle's room is on," he explained…relieving me further.

"Your name…you must have descendants from the Mideast or around those parts," I inquired taking advantage of his mentioning a relative.

"Yes, my mother and father were both from around Pakistan. They moved to this country to join me while I was a student at John Hopkins. A sister, Kahli, preceded me to the U.S. and settled in the Twin Cities. She worked for a medical device firm before succumbing to cancer. She married a Jerold Smythe and had a daughter…the daughter being Sylvia."

I was taking notes, of course, as he told me about himself. He said he also studied and worked at the famous Cleveland Clinic before accepting a research and department head position at Mayo in Rochester. Oddly enough, one of his specialties even focuses on REM dreams.

I heard enough to convince me that he indeed was qualified to bring Al out of his coma. My only regret was not getting in touch with him sooner and giving him the go-ahead to get my uncle on his feet again, and of course enable him to continue his investigative reporting on drug dealing, smuggling and a variety of other criminal activities that he was so good at uncovering with his interesting newspaper stories.

Assured that doctor Lahn would be giving me an encouraging report on Al in the very near future, I was now able to continue my local police work at a somewhat more relaxed pace without wondering what was happening to him in the hospital.

My attention was turned on getting more information from state criminal records and contacts of that youth killed downtown. His name was Leonard Kapin, only 19 who surprisingly had a fairly impressive resume as a student and hard worker. He apparently came from good parents who sent him to the best schools. Further checking, however, showed that he did have a little record at times for getting into trouble at a few bars and the like around town.

But his positive report far exceeded any negatives. It seems he was interested in becoming a lawyer and often volunteered as a paralegal aid whenever possible. He had many compliments included in his personnel files, noting that he did a fine job and had a good attitude.

He was so liked, in fact, that I almost yawned reviewing his records. That is until I spotted another name toward the end of the report. The name hit me like lightening. I looked at it twice, each time asking myself: what in hell is John Elroy doing in this guy's personnel file?

But there it was. The victim of this shooting also worked as an intern in the office of the "honorable" city councilman J.P. Elroy. What he did as an intern could cover a lot of things, I'm sure, from running errands, assisting promotion, even lighting Elroy's cigars. But what made me wonder most was: did he have anything to do with this politician's suspected drug running operations...or representing this big shot in meetings or encounters with others also involved with drugs?

Still wondering about all this, I met again with my pal Charley McKay of our narcotics squad to hear what he might also know about the late Leonard Kapin. He was just passing by my cubicle and I tried to act nonchalant when inquiring about this, remembering that the editor of Al's paper didn't want word to get out yet on Elroy. So I just matter-of-factly mentioned Kapin.

"Kapin, Kapin..." Charley mumbled, trying to recall any guy he's met with that name. "I think I might have known his old man, Arnie Kapin. But Arnie's been in the cooler for many years. Come to think of it, he did have a son...just a little guy when I met him at his father's trial. Couldn't figure out why anyone would allow a youngster to hear about the crime his daddy was accused of."

"And what was that?...was it drugs?"

"And then some. He was also mixed up in prostitution, fraud, and you name it. His wife found out about it and divorced him. But then she also got into lots of trouble with a slime ball in the gambling rackets up here and ran off with him to Vegas...leaving the kid almost alone."

Chapter 14

Poor guy, I thought, maybe he's better off where he is...wherever that is. At least he probably won't be alone anymore considering all the unfortunates who become criminals hooked on drugs and end up so tragically. I wasn't able to dwell on this very long, however, since McKay approached me again—this time with a message that the chief wanted to see me. I thought this strange, since the chief usually just drops by my desk to casually chat about matters relating to my investigations—no 'behind the door' type discussions.

Whatever he wanted I had a gut feeling that it would be important and perhaps very private. My hunch was right when he got up from his desk and closed his office doors as soon as I entered. Indicating that I should sit down, he quit smiling and his expression suddenly turned stern and very serious.

"Joe, I don't know why…but I've been asked by my higher-ups in the city to have you spend more time investigating reported corruption in our tax system. Seems there's been some problems regarding numerous city taxpayers cheating on their taxes. I know this isn't what you're used to, but they feel a good detective is needed to find out what's going on."

I almost began laughing. Me?...the guy who relies on his wife to do his taxes and as a kid had a hard time with simple arithmetic. I'm selected to help the tax department?

"Who the hell wants me to do that? I'm up to my eyeballs in real criminal cases."

The chief frowned too, saying "yes, I know...it doesn't make much sense. As to who asked for this—it comes right from the office of an important city councilman."

"Let me guess—John P. Elroy."

The chief seemed startled by my guessing ability. He also appeared caught off-guard and flushed a little before continuing.

"Joe, you're not supposed to know anything about this. In fact, the less said the better. Just consider this a compliment that you were the one selected. They must regard you very highly to want your help with such important investigation."

Although somewhat lost for words, I stood up and looked the chief right in the eyes, asking—"And what if I refuse?"

The chief remained calm, removed his glasses in thought, and then said: "Why don't you think it over first? This guy Elroy is a real heavyweight in the city power system. He could have my job as well as yours."

I had to control both my temper and the urge to tell the chief what I thought about Elroy, and the information my uncle has on him. Recalling my promise to both Terry and Al's editor I nearly bit my lip to prevent letting the chief know what's been going on with that councilman-and the scoop Al has been writing for his paper. Not knowing what to say, I simply walked out muttering: "Okay, but I'm not a tax snoop."

I took my frustration over this stupid assignment home with me and Sarah could quickly tell I was in no mood to be playful with Maddie and the pup, nor spend much time loving my wife. I was grumpy and made my new extra job the topic of conversation at the dinner table.

Fortunately, Sarah was a good and patient listener. She also was puzzled over why I got such a "dumb" assignment. Without going into this much with her and keeping my promise not to discuss the Elroy matter, I tried to turn to more cheerful topics—namely the hopefully brighter outlook for Al now that all obstacles were now seemingly removed for doctor Lahn and his special medical expertise to help my uncle get out of that deep sleep he's been in for so long.

Most of the evening, I remained close to the phone expecting Lahn to be calling me at any moment about Al's health status. When no calls came, and it was almost midnight, I went to bed still rather grumpy, wondering why the hell the doctor is taking so long to let me know if everything went well with his treatment of Al. And even though I was in the mood for loving my sexy wife, I knew I had to have a good night's sleep to tackle that damn tax job facing me in the coming days.

Despite a restless night, I was up and at 'em bright and early after getting out of bed, and so hungry that I almost forgot I still hadn't heard from doctor Lahn. I wondered why?

In fact, all day long I wondered why I wasn't hearing from Lahn. It even interrupted my startup work on that damn tax investigation case I was asked to pursue, although that didn't bother me very much since my heart wasn't into that at all. But my heart was certainly into wanting to assist my uncle, which is why I kept looking forward to hearing from the doctor nearly all day long.

When I couldn't stand waiting for Lahn's call any longer, and needing a break from that tax project, I grabbed my cell phone and hurriedly clicked onto his phone at the hospital. All I got was his voice telling me he wasn't available right now but to please leave a message. I tried again and again intermittently to catch him when I could, but to no avail. You might say the doctor was indeed out.

My final resort before quitting time, was to call the main number of the hospital. Surely they keep track of doctors or at least know their schedules. When I got through to the receptionist I was put on hold for what seemed like half-an-hour as she tried contacting Lahn. I almost fell asleep listing to the background music.

My heart seemed to skip a beat when she finally came back to the phone and said, "Mr. Kavinsky, I'm sorry but no one seems to know where doctor Lahn is right now. I understand he hasn't been seen in the hospital all day."

"Did he leave any message? Do you know where I can reach him? It's quite important."

She paused for a few minutes and then replied, "No, I'm sorry, no one knows where he's at. Sometimes the doctors are called away by emergencies."

Yeah, and what could be more of an emergency in my mind now than the life of my uncle. At first I thought there could be a mixup because he wasn't a regular staff physician at the hospital, but after thinking it over he must have been known somewhat around that hospital since they had no great problem in knowing that he was missing.

In other words, there was nothing I can do...but was there? That question came to mind when figuring out my next attempt. The answer was to quickly call Terry Johnson in hope that maybe the DEA caught something on their surveillance cameras or mirrors that could help locate Lahn. After all, he was intending to help Al as soon as he could, perhaps he was in Al's room for that matter.

But my hope nearly gave way to despair after clicking onto Terry's cell phone. Terry had nothing new to report since the doctor hadn't visited Al night or day since the last time he was seen on camera or mirror.

"Try contacting his niece, the nurse. She should know. My God, a well-known doctor like Lahn can't just disappear. He'd leave word where he could be reached I'm sure," said Terry. He hesitated then, and I wondered why, until he remarked—"unless he's ran into foul play…like someone who may not want him to wake up."

That got me thinking of who that might be. Elroy was top on my list, of course, followed closely by relatives of Frankie Frenole, but there could be others…then again, Lahn may have overslept or just plain got tired of this whole mess and took off.

Not waiting for answers to come from someone else, I immediately took it upon myself to check things out personally. That meant hopping into my squad car and speeding to the hospital with lights flashing. When I arrived, I'm sure some bystanders looked as though I was going to stop at the emergency room entrance. Instead, I surprisingly found a spot to park in the usually crowded entranceway and nearly ran into the reception area and caught the elevator going to Al's floor before its doors could close.

In my haste I also almost bumped into Sylvia the nurse. She was walking rather nonchalantly down the corridor with a stethoscope around her neck on the way to the nurses' desk in the center of the wing where Al was. I quickly asked her where doctor Lahn could be found. Blushing somewhat upon hearing his name, she told me she hadn't seen him for a few days. I knew that was wrong, since only yesterday morning Terry gave me his report on her and the doctor kissing behind closed doors.

"When's the last time you saw him with my uncle? He was supposed to be checking on him as soon as possible." She said, "I know, someone told me you called about this earlier today...I'm sure he's just been detained for a brief time and should be here shortly. Your uncle is about the same-no worse nor better. If you want, I'll have doctor Lahn paged...he may be near."

Chapter 15

▼

Urging Sylvia to page Lahn, I told her to tell him to see me in Al's room and continued to check on my uncle while listening to the loud page announcement being made around the hospital for the "missing" doctor Lahn.

When I entered the room, still somewhat dark without the lights on, I encountered someone bending over my uncle—it wasn't Lahn, but it was someone I met before. Yes, it was the mysterious health advocate Marlis who seemed to be mumbling some prayers.

She looked up, smiling as though waiting for me, saying softly, "Your uncle is still in dream land Mr. Kavinsky." She added, "Do you know anything about dreams?"

Without giving me a chance to reply, the hooded lady continued, "Researchers say we're born to be dreamers. In fact, they believe almost the entire state we're in even before being born is what they call REM sleep which they say is characterized by intense brain activity and rapid eye movement."

"Eye movement in a baby? sounds strange."

"Yes, researchers believe brain activity during REM resembles that of the waking brain." She added, "Most dreaming occurs during REM. Your uncle has been in this condition for a long time. I'm sure he'll have some very interesting things to tell you when he's awake."

"*IF* he wakes up," I commented with my fingers crossed for luck.

"Oh, but he will. There have been many prayers said for him I'm sure. He apparently is receiving excellent attention from doctors."

This led to my asking her if she knew any of these doctors, and if doctor Lahn was one of them.

"I only know doctor Frenole. He was outside the room with another doctor whom I never met, but he may have been doctor Lahn. They were talking about something I couldn't hear or understand...indeed they almost seemed to be arguing and I sensed that both were becoming upset."

"Did they come into the room?"

"No—I believe they must have had some difference of opinions and perhaps went to a more private place to discuss the matter. They both seemed very interested in the condition of your uncle, however, and I don't believe you should be concerned about not having good doctors looking out for him."

To emphasize this, she noted the new respiratory and morphine alert devices now in the room. But when she listened closely to Al's breathing she said there was very little improvement.

She sighed a little. I couldn't help but think that she was over-acting, being too dramatic...almost a little phony.

"This poor man shouldn't die from a drug overdose while receiving treatment for drugs," she declared sadly. "It could very well be happening. As an advocate I've already voiced my concerns with the hospital."

Taken back by this sudden change from hope to nearly despair, I asked: "Do you think someone has been giving him more narcotics than he needs?"

"No, but it could be that he has many times the lethal dose of morphine in his blood. Frankly, although I'm sure our prayers are helping him, he seems to be sinking deeper and deeper into his coma."

"You aren't as optimistic as you were at first, are you?"

She sighed again, saying "If only he showed some improvement. Maybe that's what those doctors were discussing. Who knows, this could even stir up a lawsuit for the hospital and attendants."

"As a health advocate and pro-activist, are you going to get to the right people for some answers? I want my uncle out of here if there's some monkey business going on."

She looked at me with a frown as though I was talking nonsense and responded, "I'm only a tiny voice in this medical center which is controlled by so many with much louder voices."

"Well, do you think my uncle's brain is being damaged by all this?"

"Takes a doctor to determine that…it would be truly a blessing if your doctor Lahn could be found for some professional answers."

Still hearing the paging going on intermittently for Lahn outside Al's room, I left the room to find nurse Sylvia in case she might know if there's been any progress in trying to locate either Lahn or Frenole.

"Last I heard they were seen going out of the hospital together. We checked with doctor Frenole's assignment desk and were told he wasn't scheduled for anything today. Usually he hardly has a free moment to himself with all the patients waiting for him," she said with a shrug.

Wondering who to turn to next, I even called up the Rochester clinic to find out if doctor Lahn was scheduled for something there today, thinking perhaps some other emergency suddenly came up requiring his special skills. Receiving no to all my questions where Lahn may be, I returned to my precinct confused over who else to contact to help explain the mysterious disappearance of this noted doctor. And why was he arguing outside Al's room?

Chapter 16

▼

I figured it was about time I called my buddy Johnson and snuck a call to him despite the chief's watching me and intermittently looking at his watch. I realized I was cutting it short since in a few minutes I was scheduled to meet with him again and go through some of the background information he has on that damn tax case.

I was lucky enough not to be put on hold and heard Terry ask, "What now old pal.?"

"Gotta talk fast, the chief's pushing me to get on a different assignment he gave me because of political pressure by Elroy. The whole thing stinks. But my main purpose for calling is because I still can't find doctor Lahn." I then updated him on my conversations with the nurse and health advocate and asked for any advice he can offer.

"Whoa! You were what by Elroy?" Terry almost gasped, as though putting the Lahn matter aside. "He must be putting the pressure on you. But how would he know you were in on what he's been doing? Someone's ratting on you behind your back, Joe. Who else would know about this besides you, me, and your uncle and editor?"

Assuring him that it was a mystery to me, too, I then tried quickly steering the conversation back to Lahn, hoping that my update would shed a little more light on the subject. Unfortunately it didn't. However, he did suggest getting immediately in touch with doctor Frenole to ask him directly what the argument was about and how come Al is still comatose?

"At this point, you've gotta be very up front with that guy. I still don't like his name…the Frenole family has been involved in so many drug problems," Terry emphasized.

Keeping this in mind, as well as the chief still staring at me impatiently, I called the hospital and asked to speak to doctor Frenole. When told he wouldn't be available until later that morning I left a voice mail telling him I'll be in his department at 11 a.m.—and would like to see him regarding my uncle.

Thinking this would give me time to discuss my new duties with the chief, I obediently heard him out about the tax corruption matter and suggested plans to investigate it. I also let him know I'm trying to do a good investigation of that drug shooting I've been checking out. This took me off the hook, so to speak, and after doing some of this spade work, I was able to leave the precinct on time for discussion with doctor Frenole, hoping of course that he got my voice mail.

Although arriving early at the hospital, I thought it indeed strange that I would be bumping into doctor Frenole walking down the entrance hospital steps that I was going up—as though rushing to depart somewhere. He didn't recognize me at first when I stopped to remind him about our scheduled meeting.

He seemed irritated, as though he hadn't heard of any meeting, and let me know he was in a hurry to get to a very important emergency. At this point I seized his arm and said angrily:

Chapter 17

"Look doc, you're not going anywhere until you talk to me about my dying uncle!"

Startled, he yanked his arm from my grasp and said haughtily, "How dare you talk to me like this. Your uncle is getting along all right, there's no need to be so rude. Where do you get the authority to approach me like this?"

"Oh, have you forgotten?—I'm a cop as well as a nephew. In fact, I'm also a detective who specializes in drug related cases—and I believe what's taking place with my uncle falls under that description." Before he could respond, I continued, "And where has doctor Lahn gone? I understand you two were heard arguing outside my uncle's room."

I could see by the expression on his face that he was greatly surprised by my mention of Lahn. He hesitated, apparently trying to come up with an answer as his face began to flush.

"I don't know anything about that man. All I do know is that he has no right to be shoving me aside from helping your uncle. Certainly I was upset over this—after all I'm only looking out for the best interest of your uncle, and I'm not sure where that doctor's coming from."

Noting that Lahn has all the proper authority to be helping, I again asked him bluntly, "Where is he?. After your argument, what happened to him? Do you know where he went?"

"You know where I'd like him to go, of course," he said arrogantly. "But hopefully he's high-tailed it back to where he came from. What he's been doing for your uncle I don't know, nor do I care because it doesn't mean anything."

I jumped on this. "It means he's trying to save him!...more than your efforts show. As a Mayo clinic specialist he's checked my uncle out and has already implemented some of the treatment he said Al needs to snap out of this coma before it's too late."

Startled by my sudden outburst, Frenole stepped back so fast he almost tripped on the steps. He could only respond with an indignant "Har-rumph."

I left him with that attack, but only after flashing my police badge and reminding him to let me know immediately if he hears anything about where Lahn can be reached.

My day's load didn't lighten up any when I got back to my desk. That murder of the young guy downtown was becoming more tied in with Elroy every time I explored the situation. The shooter was unknown, but looking over some of the councilman's assistants surprised me somewhat since a few were charged with drug running in the past, although none went to court. I asked myself why?...and how did they get the okay to be on his staff?

I met with the chief to get some answers, but he seemed as befuddled about all this as I am. He seemed worried, however, although he answers to the mayor, and not to a councilman.

I also took advantage of the meeting to tell the chief my need to talk directly to Elroy. I made it sound as though this would focus mainly on the young man's shooting, having been informed that it may be linked to some council staffers, and to the tax case which Elroy seems so interested in. By so doing, I thought, this could also cloak my real reason for talking to him—namely to find out any clues as to the whereabouts of Lahn and to even gently probe a little into Elroy's connection with the Frankie Frenole family.

The chief bought it—although he stressed he'd rather have my first priority be how I might handle the tax case best and those people he thinks I should be questioning.

With this official go-ahead, I phoned Elroy's office and asked to be scheduled to visit with him briefly regarding the tax case he wanted me to investigate. I sort of knew this would be okay since after all it was his request that this be done, probably to throw me off any further investigation of his possible role in preventing Al from doing his story on the councilman's drug involvement.

After being put on hold, which I was getting used to by now, his secretary returned to the phone to let me know her boss was interested in seeing me—and would this afternoon be okay? I was somewhat surprised by his desire for such a meeting so quickly. For some reason, however, it made me even more suspicious than ever of this guy. I couldn't help but be concerned about what he may up to? And is he possibly aware of what I may be up to? Most of my morning was spent on figuring out my best approach when meeting him.

Elroy's office was in the heart of downtown, in fact even close to the drug shooting. I was impressed by his fancy headquarters to a point where I thought I should have put on my best looking suit. But it didn't matter much how I looked, nor that I was pre-scheduled to see him, since his secretary seemed to be automatically directing visitors to chairs near her desk.

Considering I was the last to check in among those waiting, I was quite surprised when my name was quickly called notifying me that "his honor" was able to see me. It was just after I had reached for an out-dated magazine near my chair while looking forward to finally being able to relax.

Entering his oak-paneled office which fit in so well with his ritzy-looking surroundings and the big desk he sat behind, I almost felt like kneeling down first before daring to speak to him. I got over this quickly, however, when he arose with a big smile and shook my hand. My first thought was to be on guard cause this guy's indeed quite a polished politician, shifty but smooth—very, very smooth.

Before I could tell him the reason for my visit, Elroy immediately thanked me for accepting his request to investigate any and all possible corruption that may be occurring among some of the city's tax counselors affecting his constituents. I listed intently, although hoping he would shut up and let me get a word in edgewise. He went on and on about how and why an investigation should be made, and held his hand up if I tried to say anything. My chance finally came when his secretary interrupted to remind him about an appointment he made.

Chapter 18

I quickly asked Elroy who he suspects in the tax case. Keeping his pompous attitude, he avoided the question. He emphasized his personal role in this and wanted to make sure I had his name and title correct. I'm sure he wanted to be regarded as a leader in the fight to protect the tax payers. I felt like he mistook me for my newspaper uncle to get his name in the headlines.

I pretended to take notes, but after minutes went by and my arm got tired I interrupted by remarking what a wonderful view he had of the downtown. He stopped talking only long enough to take another puff of his cigar. But he did take time to turn his chair around to look at the panoramic scene the large picture window provided.

This gave me the chance to bring up the shooting. "Too bad the view was marred somewhat by the awful shooting of that kid the other day."

Elroy stopped smoking, and coughed a little before saying "I hadn't noticed, was there a shooting detective?"

"Yes, a very bad one. Some young fella got killed. We understand it was because of drugs. When you deal with that, of course, you're often dealing with death."

Elroy coughed again, looking at his watch indicating he wanted to resume his talk on possible tax corruption. However, I figured this was the time to talk about the shooting and to try focusing on what he may know about it. I had to be direct so I put on my most serious detective frown and asked him directly if he might know anything about this shooting since there were some rumors floating around that some of his associates may have been involved, directly or indirectly.

I hit a nerve…and could see him become suddenly flustered and a little red in the face, almost like taking the wind and smoke out of his sails.

He didn't respond at first. Only after he snuffed out his cigar, sat back in his over-stuffed chair, and took off his glasses did he seem to know what to say.

"I'm not too worried about what's going on around me, but am very concerned about what can be helpful for the people I'm responsible to protect. You're a very good detective, Joe, one who was highly recommended to me by those who know you…which is why I selected you for this tax corruption probe."

Wow…what a slick way to get past the shooting discussion. But I couldn't let him do that…I had to continue with that subject or walk away no closer to solving my uncle's problem than I was before meeting this guy. I was hoping he'd try to defend himself and point to some reasons why he believed crime was escalating so much that it was even outside his door, so to speak. But he side-tracked all this, so I had to be even more direct this time staring him in the eyes and asking him outright—"Sir, once again—do you know anything about this killing?"

Hearing these words from my mouth also made me feel somewhat guilty about maybe breaking my promises not to accuse Elroy yet about any wrongdoings. I could tell by his expression that perhaps I may have, but only time will tell.

He arose from his chair, put his glasses back on, and returned my stare. I expected some further discussion, but from what I could tell he was all through with our conversation.

"I have another person to see Mr. Kavinsky. Again, I wish you well with your detective work on that tax matter. Stay on it, and I'll expect a report from your chief in the near future."

I tried to avoid any confrontation with this egotistical bastard, but just stared back at him and said softly, "You'll be hearing from me, I'm sure…one way or the other."

"Let's hope it's all affirmative. If you need any help, let me know. We've just gotta catch those rascals undermining our tax system."

I asked, "How about undermining our society…with drugs?", feeling I just can't leave this creep thinking he won our conversation. My detective sense told me that indeed this guy is guilty up to his bushy eyebrows.

He smiled again and waved farewell. Before I closed the door, however, he looked at me and asked with a sneer, "By the way how's your uncle doing these days…I heard he's sick."

I didn't respond, but sure felt like giving him the' bird' finger when departing. If he thought the topics we covered were finished he had another thought coming.

My thoughts, though, were still primarily on uncle Al. I still hadn't heard anything about doctor Lahn, and anger began welling up in me rather than concern thinking why the hell Lahn wouldn't get in touch with me by now. Was he ignoring me?…was he also trying to quiet Al?

Figuring I may never know the answers to all this, I nearly accepted defeat driving back to my precinct. It wasn't until my cell phone beeped that I escaped from this funk. It was from Terry with some good news for a change.

"We think we're on the track to finding doctor Lahn. Last heard he was staying with a resident of the hospital. Don't know yet if he's there willingly or as a captive, however.
We're assigning some of our guys to round him up. The house where he's expected to be is a small place near the university campus. We believe the fellow he's with is a medical student working toward a specialty like Lahn's"

"When do you think you'll have him?"

"Can't say for sure, but knowing the urgent condition of your uncle it should be very soon. We'll be sure to speed it up, Joe…rely on us. In the meantime, what's new with you?" He asked like he knew I may be checking into other related matters, like talking to Elroy.

Chapter 19

I leveled with Terry, knowing that he, above all, should be able to keep a secret. Describing my meeting with Elroy, I expressed my negative feelings about him, including those relating to the killing of the young drug dealer.

"My gut tells me this guy had something to do with that and is sitting back laughing at us in our attempts to help Al. He claims he knows nothing about Lahn, however. I don't believe him. Do you have some words of wisdom on any of this—mister smart DEA genius?"

"Only that the DEA will be checking into it. Like you, the first priority should be finding Lahn for your uncle's sake. In the meantime, we'll quietly do our thing. We'd like to catch that bastard just as much as you do."

My mind was cluttered with all this when I finally left work for home where I can always find my reclining chair and get some much needed rest. Sarah made me extra comfortable, even putting a pillow behind my neck as I stretched out on the recliner. And she made sure Maddie and the dog stayed far enough away that their occasional shouting and barking wouldn't disturb me. I fell into a deep sleep, dreaming about the time when as a young boy my uncle and I went fishing in northern Minnesota. I accidentally fell from the canoe we were in and as I splashed about to avoid being washed away by the strong current he dove in after me. I was a poor swimmer and he wasn't much better, but he had longer arms and was able to reach out and pull me aboard as the boat almost overturned.

Hell, I'm sure if it wasn't for my uncle watching over me I probably would've drowned. But the more I think of it, I'd at least be away from the terrible crime and murder I so often encounter in my line of work. I could hardly recall any of the details about my dream when I awoke, which made me once more wonder if Al will remember anything about his coma—that is, if he can successfully pull through the 'dreamland' he may still be experiencing.

The damn phone next to my recliner woke me abruptly from my dreams. Sarah had thought of nearly everything to keep things quiet during my nap except for disconnecting the nearby phone that's equipped with a sound enhancer device to hear better for my police work. It makes such loud noise when someone calls that I almost jumped when it went off. In fact, I was at first puzzled over where the hell the noise was coming from, before realizing the room I was in wasn't the bedroom but my so-called office where I occasionally used my computer.

When I did grab the phone about all I could hear was a whisper. Usually the device on the receiver could pick up almost any sound no matter how low or muffled. By pushing my ear very close to the receiver I could finally make out some of what was being said.

"Mr. Kavinsky, it is I—doctor Lahn. I can't talk long. I fortunately located this phone where I'm at. I've been wanting to get back to you, but feel like I'm prevented from doing so." This got me to sit up in a hurry, and I motioned to Sarah not to come into the room while I'm talking when she opened the office door to ask who's calling. I then listened intently to be sure of what I'm hearing…wondering if this man's being held captive?

"Where are you for God's sake?" is the first question I could think of.

"I'm not sure what the address is, but I'm with doctor Frenole."

"But you're expected to be with my uncle, trying to save him. You indicated you were going to rush to his bedside the last time we talked."

"I know…your uncle has only two more weeks until he's brain damaged. But on my way to his hospital room I was met by doctor Frenole who said it was urgent that I talk with him about some procedures he had in mind to further help your uncle. I thought it best to hear about this. Although I already made some improvements on your uncle, he said it would be best if I go to his private lab close by so he can fully explain and show me how effective his treatment is."

"Can you come right now to Al's room?" he urged.

"I'm trying to, but every time I attempt to go Frenole has some other topics to talk about. He knows my need to hurry, but I feel he's going out of his way to delay me."

"Does he have anyone else with him who might help you?" I asked. He replied, "No, we seem to be alone—but since I'm new to the area I don't know how to be helped except by you. Fortunately, you left your office and phone numbers with me. The more I see Frenole the more I think he might even do me harm if he knows I'm talking to you."

Quickly asking if he can at least describe where he's at—his surroundings or any type landmark that could help me find him—I remembered the phone number he's calling from may be on my phone monitor like many other numbers I've been receiving lately. With no other way to trace him, I clicked onto the monitor and sighed in relief when seeing the phone number he was using.

Jumping from my comfortable chair, I warned him not to try fleeing but to remain calm because I'm sure I can track him down. I also cautioned him not to mention to Frenole that he phoned me. I was sure he could be located by way of the phone number I was able to bring up.

For any other way to find him, I left that up to Terry. I immediately called him, even though it was after office hours for him, too. But hell, I figured, these DEA guys get big bucks for keeping alert and ready for emergencies at nearly all times.

Despite all this, however, Johnson still came to his phone a little cranky. "Hey, pal, don't you know it's dinner time?" was his only greeting for me.

"Can't wait partner. Just got a call from doctor Lahn. He seems to be in mighty big trouble trying to get back to help my uncle in the hospital. He claims doctor Frenole has been delaying him and wonders why. He really sounds sincere in wanting to break loose from Frenole so he can return to rescuing Al immediately…if not sooner." My voice began trembling realizing the short time we had to help free Lahn.

"Do you know where we can find him, Joe?"

"Not exactly, but my phone monitor does. I take it you guys can search that number so it can lead right to him."

"Okay, okay," Terry almost shouted as he urged me to tell him the numbers . Once he got them, he told me that this was probably enough to find both of those mysterious doctors.

He also assured me that he's been checking out Elroy, even to the point of focusing on some of his private life. His final words on the phone, before hurriedly clicking off, were: "You'd be amazed at what we're finding out so far.

"But I'll let you know when the time is right. In the meantime 'mum's' the word. This man can be full of revenge as we all should know by now."

I kept those words in mind, although I couldn't remove from my mind the desperate rush needed to keep my uncle breathing. The ugliest thought was that he might already be brain dead from lack of sufficient oxygen.

Such thoughts overwhelmed me, so much so that I felt it necessary to go to Al's room again, knowing, however, I couldn't do anything to help him. But just the desire to see him and hold his hands was a good reason. That's what I told Sarah as I prepared to depart for the hospital.

My wife insisted that she go along, explaining we could leave Maddie off with aunt Kay, who seems to always want to baby-sit her, and my aunt's home is on the way. Plus, Sarah was sure Kay would appreciate knowing our opinion—as unprofessional as it is—how Al is doing.

Visiting my aunt Kay's is sad these days, but hopefully little Maddie will cheer her up. It is obvious that my aunt has aged greatly since her husband's coma. In fact, her arthritis is acting up so much that it's difficult for her to get around—much less to Al's hospital room. And she was now limping and sometimes needed a cane.

A devout Catholic, Kay squeezed a rosary in my hand when she said goodbye as we departed, leaving Maddie in her arms. We knew it was for the best, and that Kay could be counted on to keep her eyes on our energetic 2-year-old.

I held the rosary beads all the way to the hospital and even in Al's room. Once we got by the guard Terry had posted at the entranceway, Sarah and I started to recite it until interrupted by a student nurse who said she was checking some of his vital signs. I caught her name, Theresa, on the badge she wore. She appeared still in her teens and had a somewhat difficult time taking Al's blood pressure reading. It was apparent she was still learning the basics but apparently had the credentials to get by the guard at the door.

I asked how Al was doing. She shrugged as though it's anyone's guess and simply replied "About the same." But we could hear her sigh as she left the room mumbling "That poor man."

Both Sarah and I kept looking down at Al, touching his warm forehead and making sure the pillow and other bedding appeared to be tucked in and okay. There wasn't really much we could do but continue praying for him and wondering how much longer he can last like this. I couldn't help thinking, boy I'll never go in for a shoulder injury like Al's...no matter how simple and safe they say it will be.

We brought back a very somber report on Al to his anxious wife. She was almost wringing her hands as we described how he appeared, hooked up to those devices and breathing heavily. I could again notice the few things doctor Lahn had accomplished on his initial checkup, before being so rudely interrupted by Frenole. At least the morphine alert wasn't sounding so I presumed his breathing was better and, hopefully, his oxygen intake. And, as I recalled, he was also given Lahn's recommended Narcan medication.

After gathering up Maddie and some treats Kay had for us in the way of cookies and candy, we headed back home. Expecting to once more relax, I had just finished reading the paper from the point I had left off when I read the story about the young lad being killed downtown. There was no reference, however, who the shooter might be nor anything regarding suspects.

I kept in mind, however, that Terry and his fellow agents were closely investigating the possibility of some Elroy connection...which helped put me at ease, especially after a hearty dinner and some more running around with our energetic little girl. Indeed, I was even so relaxed that I made some passionate love to my ever-lovely wife at bedtime. She couldn't resist, indicating she also wanted to forget the sadness of the day and take in the goodness of our love-making. But despite all this, my dreams that night were more on Al and the evil circling around him…they were more like nightmares.

Despite my mostly restless night, I was out of bed shortly after sunrise with positive thoughts about how important it is to keep my body in shape for the many times a cop should be ready to handle tough, mean-spirited criminals. My police hand-book emphasizes the need for exercise and I'm just fortunate enough to have an excellent fitness club near our neighborhood.

Besides, I thought, jogging around the track and lifting weights would be a welcome relief from the many depressing things happening to me lately. I felt so intent on getting to the club that I almost forgot catching a cup of coffee, a small pack of ready-to-eat oatmeal, and a banana I spotted on the kitchen counter. I also took time to write a little note to Sarah telling her where I'm going…with a PS:*I LOVE YOU* scribbled at the bottom. I taped it on the microwave so she would be sure to see it.

Rushing to the club probably brought my blood pressure up, but the workout I was planning should bring it back down I'm sure. Getting in the swing of things, I grabbed the bar bells to make certain my muscles were still ready for action, and after many ups and downs with thoseI went to the apparatus designed to strengthen most of my upper body by enabling me to stretch my arms and torso forward and backward in sync with some loud exercise music.

Chapter 20

▼

The exercise all felt great, although I knew I'd be sore and stiff on my return to the precinct. It was while I was changing back to my work clothes that I noticed someone who seemed familiar. Yeah, by golly, it was the guard at Al's room. I was all set to chat with him, but he turned away and strolled from the locker area without noticing me. I hurried to finish dressing and dashed out the door to meet him. However, he was already at a meeting with some guys in a very secluded area…Surprisingly, one of them was none other than John Elroy.

The guard! I thought with my mouth open. The guard!…why the hell haven't I suspected the guard to be involved in this until now?. For that matter he could have allowed any spook around to enter Al's room. What's more, he probably knows all the devices Terry installed to catch those coming and going. In fact, he could have turned them off without anyone knowing.

With all this in mind, I hesitated to interrupt their meeting but instead remained out of sight wondering what they were talking about, and to see if I recognized anyone else. There was a woman involved as well as three other men. She looked somewhat familiar but the rest were strangers to me. I know I met her somewhere before—but where?

As I tried to figure all this out I was bumped by a fat guy who wasn't looking where he was going while departing from the club. He still was almost wringing wet from his workout and had a grumpy look as though he was having a hell of a time trying to shed a few pounds from his very large belly.

Despite his mad expression, however, he was very much a gentleman…excusing himself and wondering if he hurt me in his hurry to leave. I just shook my head no and kept walking indicating that I also was in a hurry to leave this place.

In a way, I was also mad…thinking if only I had my camera. But I had nothing to show or record this mysterious meeting taking place. There it was to capture as possible evidence—and there I was without even a pencil or paper to note the time nor the exact place. All I knew for certain is that they're in one of the lounges near the entrance—but there were several of those on the main floor of the spacious club.

The big fella didn't walk off. Instead he continued to talk, mostly about his need for losing weight and what a great club this was for the variety of equipment he could use to accomplish such a tough feat.

As he talked, I noticed he had a camera. Each time he breathed it seemed his large belly wiggled, enabling me to see it on the belt barely holding up his pants. I asked about his camera and what photos he was taking in the club, since I could tell he was a camera buff—and when I mentioned this his smile became almost as broad as his big puffy face.

You could tell he was just waiting for someone to talk about cameras, probably his favorite subject. He proudly and quickly showed me his sophisticated digital camera, noting that he especially enjoys taking candid photos whenever the opportunity arose.

He explained, proudly and with a chuckle, that he took some pictures of the special equipment the club has for helping to take pounds off big guys like him.

This, of course, gave me the opportunity to ask if he could take a picture for me. To make him feel a little indebted. I said this with a slight grimace as I felt my arm where I was bumped. He grinned, welcoming the chance to do me a favor. When he asked what the subject was, I pretended to look casually around and finally focused on the meeting taking place.

Pointing to those around the meeting table, I told him they were some friends of mine and then asked if he has a zoom that could enlarge the view and show their faces. That really turned him on—he gladly showed me his sophisticated zoom device, quickly brought the small camera in focus and began taking photos. Thank God there was no bright flash or loud camera clicking that could cause the meeting group to notice they were being photographed. It was like being on 'Candid Camera'.

In fact, his fancy camera immediately produced a photo print. He also said he'd put it on a CD disc as well as send me an email with the views he took, which would enable me to makes as many prints I might want on my own computer.

I was sort of taken back by all this, thinking I was lucky enough just having him take the picture. What could I do, other than shake his hand and thank him. He declined my offer to pay him for his effort by simply saying "no thanks—I owed you one."

I accepted the one print and sighed in relief noticing that all the faces were clear and easily seen. What a break! My DEA pal couldn't gripe that I didn't get enough information—cause there they were, all huddled together...probably talking about my poor bedridden and defenseless uncle.

After obtaining the name of this friendly photographer, I quickly jumped into my squad and took off to the precinct. I didn't want to bother Terry with his attempts to find Frenole, but I knew the photo may very well help him with his quiet investigation of the Elroy matter.

But keeping this a secret was too much even for me. I felt like a little kid eager to squeal on his big sister kissing her first boyfriend. Thinking of squealing, I heard my brakes squeal as I stopped quickly in the police ramp. Before entering the detective department, however, I thought it best to click onto Terry rather than phoning him at my desk, and hopefully avoid letting the whole department know I'm once again ignoring my regular assignments...especially that damn tax case.

Johnson reacted both surprised and somewhat skeptical when I related what I saw at the fitness center. He wasn't as pleased as I thought he'd be. You could sense that he didn't like hearing that his special guard was there. Although he didn't know the guy very well he was sure his associates checked him out thoroughly before assigning him to protect Al.

"Are you sure it was him? We didn't ask him to be with Elroy, nor did I know he even knew the councilman. I assigned that investigation to some of my other agents, not to him."

"Well, I have the photo to prove it...probably more views than needed. Can I meet with you soon?...I'd hate to lose any of this." Before he could set a time or place, I thought it was also time to ask him how he's been doing tracking down Frenole so we can hopefully get doctor Lahn to complete his special care of my uncle.

"We're moving ahead, Joe, but unfortunately this takes a little time...which I'm not sure your uncle has. That phone number you came up with was helpful in leading us to the house where Lahn made his phone call, but didn't lead us directly to him. The landlady told us everyone moved out unexpectedly without any trace. But she heard one remark that they were on the way to a home in the St. Paul Crocus Hill area. Right now our agents are checking into this. Sorry Joe, but that's all I have to report at this time."

After being once more assured I would be contacted immediately when Lahn is found, I pondered over Terry's reference to "everyone." Did that mean there's a number of people involved in keeping doctor Lahn from helping Al?

That question remained in my mind as I looked over the photo once more that the bulky fella with the versatile camera gave me. At first I thought I didn't recognize anyone other than the guard and Elroy. The more I studied it, however, the more the lady with that bunch reminded me of someone. But who could that be?

Aha! Now it suddenly came to mind. Damn! that's her—it's Marlis the health advocate.

Chapter 21

▼

I tried putting all the pieces together to figure out why this very reverent miss, with all her apparent health care knowledge and spiritual feeling for others, would be mingling with the likes of these bad apples in the photo I'm inspecting. At least I know two are rather rotten…but who's the third guy among these misfits?

Try as I might, I can't identify him. He's sitting next to Frenole and across the table from the guard. The view I have shows Elroy pointing at the doctor while the others stare at him as if agreeing what's being said…It's as though Elroy's bawling out Frenole for some reason. I shuddered to think that the reason may be because my uncle is still alive.

I had to keep myself from running to their table and turning it upside down. But I realize it's best to show the photo and discuss this with Terry when I'm in a calmer frame of mind…if that's ever possible in this rather spooky, goofy job of mine.

While still studying this photo I was startled once again. This time by a rather debonair young man who, despite being in tennis shorts, appeared like he could be on the cover of a men's fashion magazine. He was smiling as though he knew me, but he didn't. However, he did recognize one of the people in the photo I was holding. That's what caught his eyes.

"Hey, that's my partner—Tony. Good photo of him, too. I didn't know he was a member of this club. Usually he's always hanging out in his busy office."

"Tony who?" was my quick response.

"Anthony Marken—he's an attorney with me in our startup little law firm. I think I finally got to him to take off a few pounds, although it doesn't look like he's exercising too much in that picture."

I stood up to introduce myself, mentioning my name but not my occupation. After shaking my hand briefly, but vigorously, he said his name is Adam—Adam Schiltz, of the Schiltz/Marken agency in St. Paul. I hadn't heard of that firm, but then again why would I? I usually prefer avoiding lawyers, especially those who get in the way of police business.

He didn't stand around long, after mentioning he was scheduled to play some racquet ball before getting back to work. But before he departed I had the opportunity to ask if he knew anyone else in the photo. He studied it again, sort of frowning and scratching his head.

"Yeah, by golly, that's councilman Elroy."

Hell, I already knew that. But he added, "I'm sure glad Tony's talking with the big politicians—they can help make you or break you when developing your business."

We then went our separate ways—mine was immediately directed at getting to Terry with my photo information—but I continued wondering who's the fourth guy in that photo?

Because time was quickly running out for Al, I didn't want to lose any of it by going back to the precinct to mess with that damn tax project. Nor did I want to wait forever for Terry to get back to me…so I headed straight to his DEA headquarters.

I knew he'd be upset over my visiting him at his office, since as an undercover DEA agent, as well as local cop, I was ordered to stay away from there to avoid any suspicion that I have any connection with the DEA. However, I shrugged off all this, putting my interest in helping Al first and to hell with all the rest.

I even waited in the reception area for Johnson to get through with whatever he might be doing, knowing all the time that I may be easily observed there by anyone who shouldn't know of my work with the agency. But I'm afraid my cover was quickly uncovered by the receptionist when she loudly announced that Mr. Johnson is now available to see me.

Entering his office, in a rather humble way, knowing I was 'off limits,' Terry at first stared at me in his scolding manner. But instead of shaking his finger, he began smiling and said in his kidding way, "You could have at least put on a mask."

I replied, as sternly as he first pretended to appear, "There's no way Terry that I'm going to mask my concern to know what you're doing to rescue Al. Also, I brought that photo with me which may help with that. I know all their names in the photo but one. But let's hear your status report first. After all, that's why I barged in here."

Pointing to a chair for me to sit down on, Terry rather calmly updated me on trying to catch Frenole…and by so doing find doctor Lahn so he can be quickly brought back to the hospital to wake Al from his longtime coma.

He first offered me a cigarette, which I gladly accepted while watching him take a deep drag on his and blow out the smoke. His first words after that also helped to put me at ease.

"We just found the house where Frenole is, and probably at this very moment our agents are rescuing doctor Lahn from his clutches. Don't know yet, however, why he was being detained, but I do have some interesting thoughts for you on this subject."

He leaned back on his chair and then told his secretary, by way of his desk intercom, that he didn't want to be interrupted and to hold all calls until notified otherwise.

I knew from his body language that he had some serious things to tell me, and I snuffed out my cigarette to let him know I'm putting all my interest on what he was about to say.

"Joe, I haven't seen that photo yet, but I'm pretty sure I can guess who's in it. Elroy isn't acting alone on his drug projects, and you're right by suspecting he's trying to keep you and Lahn from reviving Al and doing all in his power to pull you away…like encouraging the chief to put you on a project completely removed from your regular detective work. He's very clever. But as you know we've been watching him and hopefully we'll soon have enough to arrest him."

Before I could say "soon isn't enough," he continued: "The way we see it, Joe, is that Elroy has been able to buy off our guard at Al's door and is probably now working on how to legally have Al's lifeline removed without any suspicion. Of course, he also could be attempting to get cooperation from appropriate hospital personnel."

I couldn't help but look again at the photo I was holding. What he said makes sense…a lawyer's pictured as well as the hospital healthcare advocate.

He continued, "But one thing Elroy doesn't know, at least when this picture was taken, is that we're about to grab Lahn from Frenole's grasp.

And I'm sure he'll have to do some tall explaining why this suspicious looking meeting took place."

I held my hand up to stop him from going any further. "Terry, this should be done at once. If you know where's he's at…go get him! Al can't be playing waiting games any longer."

"I know, I know…but there's lots of power players in on this, Joe, and the whole effort could blow up in our face if we don't handle this very carefully."

"Well, Marlis certainly hasn't much power, but I can't figure her role in all this. After all…I caught her praying for Al."

"Yeah, probably praying that he'll hurry up and die," Terry scoffed.

On my way out of Terry's office, I turned around before opening the door and remarked: "Promise me one thing more, when you do round them up…especially Elroy…let me have a chance at them. I've got something to settle with them all, including Frenole."

"Whoa, Joe, no fisticuffs! Please, leave this up to us. With the feds arresting him it'll mean more to the courts as well as to the press. I'll tip you off once we get them, but we'll be the ones to handle this. I know you'd like to get your hands on them, but that'd only give their lawyers some ammunition to defend those bastards.

"Don't forget you represent the cops in this case, and everyone's just waiting to come down on any so-called police brutality."

Accepting this, but keeping in mind I sure would like to punch out any and all who are slowing attempts to help Al, I said goodbye to Terry but not before I once again reminded him that I'm anxious to know immediately when the DEA catches up with any of them. As soon as I hear, of course, I'd do all I can to get Lahn back to Al's bedside.

Troubled by all this, it was extra difficult to return to that damn tax case, especially knowing that Elroy had something to do with putting me on it. While shuffling papers to see what to do first I noticed once again the report on that young shooting victim downtown. I already had the name of his parents, but the latest information on my desk also provided the name of his only brother and where he resided and worked, as well as information that he, too, has a drug history.

I quickly shoved aside the data I had on the tax matter...almost hoping it would drop into the waste basket next to my desk, and then turned my attention to getting more evidence about the shooting and its possible tie-in with Elroy.

I realized that the best way to sometimes get possible crime information is to actually meet with the person who may have it. This prompted my calling on the victim's brother, whose first name is Marcos. And just so this is done with a proper warrant and backup in case of any legal outcry or emergency, I also was accompanied by our precinct narcotics investigator and longtime pal Charley McKay when I knocked on Marcos Kapin's door in a somewhat shady neighborhood. And I don't mean shady from the trees. It was very run down with lots of poor kids playing in the littered street and tough looking guys hanging around...an ideal setting for drug dealers prying on the unfortunates.

McKay and I carefully waited for the door to open. Like me, I'm sure Mack also had his hand on a gun under his jacket. We took turns knocking on the door and ringing the bell.

We were almost ready to give up, when the creaky door slowly opened.

The guy behind the door looked upset. It was very apparent he didn't welcome any company, and this was especially noticeable when we announced we're from the police department. In fact, we almost had to push against the now half-opened door to talk with him, and made sure our badge and revolver could be seen to show him our authority to enter.

But he seemed more frightened than anything else. However, I felt this was only natural in the creepy environment surrounding him. I also felt sorry for him considering the everyday risk he faced just walking about this ungodly neighborhood and, of course, what he may be going through due to the sudden and tragic loss of his brother.

My partner and I both quickly explained the reason for our visit. Since he didn't offer us a place to sit down we continued to stand while relating our need for more information regarding why he thinks his brother was murdered and—above all—who may be the killer.

Before he began talking with us I noticed he nervously put a latch on the door, looking first to see if there was anyone else in the hallway. A pitcher of coffee was on a nearby counter, although he didn't offer us any. There was no smell of opium or any pot usually detected in places suspected of drug use. When he did talk, he did so only after carefully pausing to consider how to respond.

He replied slowly to most of our questions, but when we began inquiring about who may have been behind the shooting, and whether it was gang related, he hesitated at first…then began to speak more clearly and seriously.

"It was Elroy—my brother told me that bastard was running a drug business on the side and anyone who crossed him would be killed. If he knew I was even speaking with you guys I'd be whacked. My brother was out of work and depended on money from this big shot."

"Has he threatened you?" McKay asked.

"Not directly, but his people have."

"People—what people?" I inquired, hoping to know more about those on Elroy's pay roll.

"There's all kind of them on the street…young and old, white and black, male and female…you name it. Most don't tell their name, and they warn you to keep your mouth shut or you're dead meat."

"Like your brother?…was he going to tell on them?" McKay interrupted.

"Yeah—like him. He was fed up with the whole damn mess. In fact, he even wanted to tell a reporter about it."

I swallowed hard and almost gasped with that comment. All I could utter was, "Maybe he did." My next words came with even more difficulty, "Was the name of that reporter Al Benjamin?"

"Yeah, that sounds like him. My brother said he was from the Star and did a lot of stories on crime and what's going on…you know, like one of those investigative writers."

Chapter 22

How well I knew. As a kid I sort of idolized my uncle. I'm really surprised I didn't grow up to be a reporter rather than a cop. I almost felt like a copy boy in a news room helping my uncle when he occasionally brought some of his work home and plugged away on his old manual typewriter until finally buying a computer. He would sometimes call for me to do odd jobs, like getting some more copy paper as he tried meeting his many deadlines.

But those were years past. However I have a hunch perhaps my dear uncle is still trying to call for me—only this time to hurry up and save his life. Moreover, Kay told me he seemed constantly at his new computer recently as if he had some great news breaks.

That's why I was so quick in relaying the information obtained from Marcos to Terry. It should add greatly to the guilt of Elroy, and I could tell by Terry's reaction that this helps solidify the case against the smooth talking politician and his underworld extracurricular activities.

"If we can get this kid to testify to the comments he made to you and Charley we have it made. That could be a big 'if', however, since he may be afraid to talk about this. As you indicated he seemed scared and may clam up in court or for the press," Johnson cautioned.

I reminded Terry that Marcos already gave some of this information to Al, who must have included it in some of the newspaper copy he was working on…but not yet published. "That means we've gotta see what copy Al's editor already has…even if he thinks it's too soon."

Needless to say, asking for Al's notes and his incomplete copy on Elroy would not be easy. Fred Hanson was known to be a strict editor and staunch believer in not running a story until all facts can be completely confirmed, allowing no chance of anyone challenging it and perhaps weakening the newsworthy reputation of the newspaper. Sort of like the situation with Dan Rather and CBS, I shrugged.

But despite all this, I knew I had to at least attempt to read what Al was working on. Although Hanson gave me some rough idea about the story in progress, both Terry and I agreed we should have the chance to look it over in greater detail to hopefully incriminate Elroy and stop the damage being done by his drug network.

How to do this tactfully is the biggest hurdle I realized while taking time to stir the coffee I was sipping at the Donut Diner enroute back to the precinct. I knew Hanson would be greatly upset knowing I talked with the DEA regarding this matter. But how could I avoid him?

My answer hopefully came as I reminisced once again about my good old days as a youngster pretending to be a reporter like my uncle when he was typing stories he took home from work. The question arose, what did he do with all the paper he used for roughing up his stories? I can still see him putting them to one side or into a file or tossing them in a paper basket.

If anyone knew—it would be my aunt Kay. Al insisted his copy should be handled with special care. When he got to the newspaper office he'd often restyle and make it letter perfect.

In any case, this would give me another opportunity to visit my aging aunt and update her on the status of her husband. I had no good news about that, of course, but kept in mind the news I wanted most at this time was what Al had been writing about Elroy…before Elroy sees it.

When I arrived at the precinct I had time to call Kay to make sure she'd be home when I dropped in. She left a voice-mail saying she was busy shopping but expected to be back around dinner time. This was okay since maybe it was best to come with my wife and child to make this more a social call rather than 'business', which in this case related to the depressing, suspected criminal activities engulfing my poor defenseless uncle.

I was all set to finally delve more into the tax case when my office phone rang. I knew it couldn't be Johnson since he always called me on my cell phone with that special code 'TJ'. I hoped and prayed that whoever it was would tell me that doctor Frenole has been nabbed and doctor Lahn is back at the hospital helping Al.

I was wrong on both matters. Turns out it was a call from the hospital. The chief of staff wanted to alert me that Al's condition was lasting much too long and wondered if we had decided to turn off the life-saving equipment. I told him emphatically "hell no"—recalling from my last conversation with Lahn that Al still had maybe a week or so left before brain damage would occur. But that was a few days ago. I almost panicked when realizing this and rapidly clicked onto Terry's cell phone. But all I got was a busy signal.

With each beep of the busy signal I became more nervous knowing that time was rapidly running out for Al. It made me realize more how precious time can really be. In fact, I almost shook the phone and was tempted to holler "get the hell off it" until coming to my senses. When I did, I also stopped the urge to bang it on my desk, but instead clipped it back onto my belt near my revolver and looked about to see if anyone noticed my angry frustration.

I did see detective McKay peering at me, however...frowning and scratching his beard. He sauntered over and placed a hand on my shoulder as though to comfort me. "Joe, take it easy pal. I've been praying for your uncle and realize the suspense and anxiety you and your aunt must be going through."

Thanking him for his support, I went back again trying to contact Terry. This time I caught him. He was almost out of his office when I called and seeing the code JOKE on his monitor (the code for my cell name) he grabbed the phone, nearly out of breath, and asked: "Joe, what's up?"

"You tell me!...Al has only about five more days until he's brain dead. Have you or have you not made any progress in finding Lahn?" I demanded.

"I'm just going out the door to get him. I have agents surrounding that address you gave me...so if all goes well, we'll have both doctors Lahn and Frenole shortly. The next time you hear should be my telling you Lahn is ready to talk to you about Al."

"For God's sake Terry...I don't need to talk to him. Just tell him to get the hell over to the hospital and start reviving Al before it's too late."

I could almost feel my head sweating as I clicked off. Noticing that once again my loud talking attracted lots of attention from my colleagues, as well as the chief, I resumed reading the notes the chief gave me on the tax case. Most of the complaints in this matter came from councilman Elroy, of course. He was accusing the mayor's office of illegally mishandling city funds obtained from unnecessary taxes levied on drugs and other "important medications" by applying them toward the building of a new metropolitan city center without proper authorization.

The words seemed impressive enough, but what were they really saying? For one thing, I figured, Elroy is striking out against the mayor since word has it that he's after the mayor's job. Another reason is that he wants to remove heavy taxation imposed on the sale of drugs for his own benefit…both, of course, would open the doors he wants by giving him more city power and monetary payback from his secret connections with the drug world.

But why bother the police department with this? I tried answering this in my own mind, reasoning that it would look more unlawful if the police comes down on the mayor than his fellow city legislators, plus this would certainly stir up greater interest and controversy from the press. Many readers would be led to believe that good old Elroy is being picked on by the upstart mayor and would lend him greater support and defense if charges are ever levied on his drug dealings. Indeed, the smooth talking Elroy could play the role of a martyr.

The one big obstacle in his way, of course, is my uncle Al. He has an eye for spotting phonies. His columns and opinions have a loyal readership and this could be a threat to the sneaky ambitions of the aggressive councilman.

But I wouldn't know what Al has written so far about this guy until I can get to my aunt's house and check out my uncle's work files. My greatest fear at this point is if Elroy knows these exist. He'd do anything to destroy them…or anyone in his way for that matter.

This made me rush all the faster in reviewing those damn tax case reports. I pretty much concluded that Elroy is using the police to make him look good. Bringing in the cops, however, might very well backfire on him. At least it's making me wonder how crooked and dangerous he is. It certainly makes me want to straighten him out…with a punch on his smiling kisser.

I was still in that angry mood upon returning home and asked my wife if she had heard from my aunt recently. She hadn't for a few days and also wondered if Kay was feeling okay with Al constantly on her mind.

This gave me the opening to tell Sarah about my plans to visit Kay and very subtly ask if I might look over the recent drafts he might have been writing before his shoulder surgery. In her diplomatic manner, Sarah said she'd help me by telling Kay that I've been recalling many of my childhood days reading his copy at his house and being in awe of my uncle's journalistic skills. How could Kay say no to her nephew's memories of his hero uncle?

Chapter 23

Unless my watch is wrong, it now shows only four days left before Al is likely to become brain dead. With this in mind and regardless of what my aunt might say or do, I still am determined to see what he may have written about Elroy in his files at home.

All the preparation and concern regarding how to tactfully approach my aunt about seeing Al's copy files was unnecessary. She seemed very pleased to see us and eager to recall the times when as a kid I'd try using Al's typewriter when he wasn't looking and once in awhile would get my fingers ensnarled in the typing ribbon. One time in particular, she recalled, I left some of Al's copy so full of smudges he couldn't make out what he had typed.

Although readily agreeing to my browsing through Al's story drafts, Kay was mostly interested of course in my update on her husband. Her smile soon vanished when she learned he was still making no progress and the outlook seems so gloomy.

Sarah kept Kay busy and away from such sad thoughts by asking about some favorite recipes that only my aunt seemed to know. As they talked, I quickly found the work files and began searching for any copy that might relate to Elroy. It didn't take me long, since you could tell Al had been using these files a lot lately…some of his rough editing was still on many of the pages. It was typical of my uncle to be going over and over his copy until he was sure he told the story like it should be and, above all, was absolutely accurate. I even noticed he kept some of my childhood scribbling when I pretended to be a big-time reporter.

Reviewing all the pages made my think that Al had been working on this story for many months. Strange he never tipped me off, but I realized he and editor Hanson made a promise not to disclose any of this until the proper time—namely when charges are filed against the councilman.

The more I read the more I became overwhelmed by what I was reading. Al must have spent half of his time digging into this. I can see what Terry was saying more clearly now…that somehow, someway Elroy must have learned what Al was up to and then did everything he could to stop him. When he learned Al was about to have surgery he could have arranged to have him overdosed…and if he knew I'm his nephew and detective he would try desperately to keep me off this case.

The pieces were coming together more readily now. Every page I read was well documented. Hell, even every claim and incident was attributed to someone. Knowing my uncle, he was determined to get to the source of things and avoid anything that wasn't based on facts.

But still, some of the prominent names and places mentioned caused me to wonder how even Al was able to find out all this. Could he have had an inside source?…someone not afraid of Elroy and secretly providing my uncle information on what's going on behind the scenes with that crafty politician. But who could that be? Perhaps he was even at Al's house as the story drafts were being typed.

While considering all this, my aunt strolled into the room with Sarah and noticed all the papers I had around me. Nodding her head sadly, she told me how often she had to clean up after her husband when he was working on a major story. It often took him a long time to proof read his first drafts and they'd be nearly all around the room.

This, of course, gave me the opportunity to ask her if Al ever had someone else with him while he was writing.

"No—never, in fact he'd get angry with me if I barged in and interrupted his train of thought. He very definitely wanted to be alone so he could concentrate better. There was only one occasion I can recall when a visitor—a young lady—came by and chatted with him recently."

"Do you know who she was?"

"Not really…Al said she was from the state department at our capitol building."

"Could you hear them talking?"

"I caught a little when I went by his room. Although the door was partially closed. I believe they were chatting about the mayor."

That makes sense. If the mayor felt that Elroy was after his job he would make sure the press got its facts correctly when mentioning him along with his opponent. For that matter, perhaps Al called the mayor's office to verify some of his information about Elroy and the mayor sent someone over to find out more what Al may have been writing. She probably was from the tax department.

But all the attributions I found so far from reading Al's rough drafts had no mention of any woman giving him information. However, I really didn't have to check into this much since my uncle included many official sources backing up the accusations in his copy. However, for what it's worth, I again asked my aunt if she recalled the lady's name.

After hesitating briefly, she snapped her fingers and said "Yes, I'm pretty sure it was Sylvia, she told me this before going into Al's office but we never had a lengthy conversation since she seemed in a hurry and their meeting was only for a few minutes."

"Sylvia what?" I asked, recalling the nurse Sylvia who I met in the hospital.

"Sorry, I can't remember. I only know she said she's from the mayor's office."

That was enough for me, realizing I could call the office to find if they have anyone named Sylvia…hoping, of course, they don't have more than one to complicate my search. I guess I heard and found enough in Al's work sheets to tell Terry about all this.

After consoling aunt Kay a bit more, Sarah and I departed and had a latte coffee shop close by where I explained further my hope and plans to get help to Al within the next 3 ½ days. I re-emphasized the need for her to let me know ASAP if she heard from doctor Lahn or anyone else regarding Al in my absence…and not to take for granted that the caller is a "good guy."

I also thought it best to click onto Terry's cell phone immediately to arrange a meeting with him to go over Al's story drafts and the people mentioned in it involving the Elroy matter. And, of course, knowing the urgency of helping Al I kept my fingers crossed in hope he had something new to report about finding doctor Lahn.

My hopes were dashed, however, when Terry told me…even before saying hello…that Lahn was nowhere in sight when DEA agents smashed down the door in the house where we thought he was being held against his will.

"But we do have Frenole…and although he claims he knows nothing about this we're now interrogating him and we're pretty sure he'll tell us where Lahn's at."

I could feel my forehead sweating again while checking my watch as time ticked off for my uncle. I was so upset that I nearly forgot another big reason for calling Terry—that Sylvia was mentioned by my aunt as a visitor to Al's home office where he was compiling evidence against Elroy.

"That's strange all right," Terry remarked. "But why would Sylvia the nurse want to talk with Al? You'd better call the tax department to see if she's employed by them. Better yet, let us do that…a government call sometimes gets the fastest answers, especially with another government agency."

"Whatever…but please do it fast. Also, don't put this ahead of notifying me if you track down doctor Lahn."

Before he clicked off, Terry asked, "I don't suppose you got the last name of this Sylvia?" He said it somewhat teasingly knowing I was caught earlier without getting the names of some of the suspects I saw in the hospital.

I stammered a bit, and then defended myself by explaining, "All I know is what doctor Lahn told me when he was caught kissing her—she's his niece, the daughter of Lahn's brother Abdul who also had a son. Sorry Terry, I dropped the ball again on this one, too."

I waited for a response, visualizing Terry getting mad. But when he did comment it was simply, "Oh, well…we'll track this down through the Minnesota Nurses Association. You did tell me she's an RN…so I'm sure she's a member of that association, as is Joan the day nurse who we've already checked out—and she's clean" Once again, I sighed in relief over this, and the DEA's forgiveness for my "failures".

Chapter 24

Only three days to go!...this was the dreadful thought in my mind when I awoke early the next morning with my wonderful wife snuggled next to me. I couldn't get very passionate, however, thinking about this and what it means for my still unconscious uncle. In fact, it kept me from sleeping most of the night.

I tried a cold shower and some push ups to refresh my mind and hopefully get back some much-needed energy for my busy work-day ahead, but nothing I could do seemed to remove those frightening thoughts of my uncle heading toward oblivion.

Even the thought of working on that damn tax case was welcomed., although this was now being shared by Terry who was checking out those mentioned by my uncle in this strange and somewhat bizarre matter. Also, I still had a newspaper clipping of that young man being shot in downtown on my desk, reminding me that I should do everything possible to catch the killer—or in this case killers.

But what really helped to wake me up was the beeping of my cell phone with "TJ" on the monitor, meaning it was from my DEA buddy Johnson again who said. "Joe—I got both good news and bad. The good is that Al's list of suspects in the Elroy case makes lots of sense and we plan to be questioning them shortly. The bad news is that we still don't know where doc Lahn is although we have been already questioning Frenole, who—I might add—is certainly not cooperating with us in any way."

"But Frenole should know, he's the one that ran off with Lahn, I noted. "Don't believe him if he tells you he doesn't. He may have even killed Lahn by now to follow Elroy's orders to keep him away from my uncle."

"I realize that, Joe. Please keep a cool head over this. There's just so far we can go with pushing him. Frenole already has his lawyer with him to cry foul nearly every time we ask him anything. He's a very wealthy physician, and can afford the best legal aid."

"Yeah—as well as lots of aid from the councilman, who is probably paying him to keep his mouth shut."

"I agree—but as a government guy I have to follow protocol, and that includes making sure our suspects are handled firmly, strictly and…gently. Believe me, I want as much as you do to smack Frenole in the choppers."

"Well, where do we go from here? This could go on forever, leaving Al brainless, or dead and even buried."

"Don't give up…although we have a bunch of suspects to still check out who seem tied in with this, I'm certain we'll clear the hurdles we're running into and make arrests. Trust me…Lahn will show up. Elroy was quite clever at putting all the right people together to achieve his goals…maybe too clever for his own good."

Almost in despair, I clicked off and began outlying some hopeful things I might do to speed things up. But there seemed to be no good answers. However, one thing Terry didn't mention was where Sylvia fits into all this. He didn't give me a report on this yet, leaving me to believe this was among all the suspects he still had left to check out.

But what the hell, I'll save him a call and contact the nurse's association to get my own information on this. I'll also contact the state tax department to see if they have a Sylvia on their employee or consultant roles. I know Terry might frown on this, but like so many governmental agencies, the DEA and state could be backlogged in bureaucracy and take forever to get this done. And Al just doesn't have that much time.

My first call was to the State Department of Taxation. It took some waiting just to get a human voice, but that's no surprise considering the bureaucrats around there. It was even longer to get a response when I asked to speak to Sylvia. When I did, the annoyed voice at the other end simply said, "Sorry there's no Sylvia on our staff."

I'm sort of speechless. There goes my theory that an insider in the department was the one at Al's house...close enough to what was going on, especially anything illegal.

This left only one other Sylvia to check...the nurse who is hopefully with the nurse's union that would be able to track her down. I used Sylvia's last name, Smythe, this time but knew this may be wrong...it didn't sound Mideast enough even though Lahn said it was.

I couldn't get through to the union office, however, and suddenly realized I read in the local newspaper this morning that the union nurses are on strike. In fact, many of the nurses are already picketing in front of many of the hospitals involved. What a hell of a time for me to expect any quick answers from them.

Just to be sure, I tried phoning the hospital administration office, but I was put on hold with a voice telling me to expect a long wait what with all the disruption caused by the lack of help relating to the strike.

Scratching my head, trying to decide what to do next, I almost slammed the phone down in frustration. The other detectives around me stared a little but were getting used to my antics since Al went into his coma.

Before I could get up from my chair and enter the men's room where I could have a little extra privacy in thinking about all this and maybe cussing out loud, my desk phone rang. The voice sounded familiar, like the guy I just got through talking to at the tax office.

It asked: "Mr. Kavinsky…you don't mean Sylvia our outside vendor?"

It's the tax guy all right. Quickly piecing this together, I replied, "Perhaps, but I thought she worked for your department and was on your staff."

"*For* the department—not *in* it'. She's one of our outside consultants. Gives us lots of good advice…like a freelancer."

He added, "Although she's not on our staff, we really rely on her a lot. She's very professional…has a degree in finance and I believe even studied law."

"What's her last name?" I asked quickly before he could hang up. I sure didn't want to goof up again with Terry by not getting complete names.

"Grabowsky, Sylvia Grabowsky. Why are you asking by the way?"

"Oh, I just may need a good consultant one of these days," I said casually with a shrug, realizing the last thing I want to do is alert anyone that the police is checking on her.

So there it is…this has to be the Sylvia that aunt Kay mentioned. I breathed a little easier knowing that there's probably no need now to continue trying to find the last name of that Sylvia in the hospital. However, I wasn't absolutely sure. Nor was I about Grabowsky.

Why was Grabowsky conferring with Al when he was working on the Elroy story? Could it be that she was an intermediary, bringing the mayor's side of the story to Al so Elroy wouldn't be the hero he wished to portray? In any case, it all seems cloaked in mystery.

At this point, I felt like just sitting back and letting all this reveal itself in its own way and time. There were so many different puzzles that it was getting impossible trying to figure it all out. But I snapped out of this immediately when thinking it could all tie in to why Al is waiting so long for help.

The characters in this scenario seemed to be multiplying daily. Thank God Terry was investigating most of them. I nearly chuckled when thinking if you put them all together in Al's hospital room there wouldn't be any room for Al.

My mix of serious and humorous thought soon vanished when the chief tapped me on the shoulder. He was frowning, usually meaning whatever I was doing wasn't good enough. I recognized that frown, especially when an investigation wasn't as fast or as smooth as he had hoped.

"How's that tax case coming, Joe? Elroy will be breathing down my throat again if I don't get back to him soon on your findings".

Knowing Chief Hermes like I do, I wasn't too surprised by his inquiry. What the hell, by now I should be leveling with him anyway and telling him what I've turned up so far. By knowing Elroy is a scoundrel he should be unwilling to do his bidding—such as taking me off my regular detective job. I'm sure he'd like to know Elroy wants to become mayor by any means possible. This should also give me more peace of mind.

CHAPTER 25
▼

Only two days left for Al…This warning kept flashing into my mind the next day after sitting down with the chief and telling him what I've turned up regarding Elroy. Plus, I had the chance to tie this into the fatal shooting of that young man downtown.

But so what? My uncle was still deep in a coma and in about 48 hours his mind will be dead.

By confiding more with the police chief, I was encouraged to even talk to him more about my uncle's condition. For one thing, now that Terry has removed his suspect agent from guarding Al's hospital door this opens the room to nearly anyone wanting to enter it.

That thought made me almost shudder thinking of who that might be. Hell, nowadays you read of horror stories…about visitors and even medical personnel giving lethal dosages of medication to intentionally kill the defenseless sick person in bed. I remember a similar incident within our precinct jurisdiction when a doctor gave a patient an overdose of digoxin, a heart medicine, that killed him within only a few hours.

The person that did this reportedly reasoned the poor patient was going to die anyway so why not make it quick and easy rather than suffering any longer. In other words, some of these do-gooders who appear to be caring for others can really be doing evil.

My God!...why hadn't I thought of that before? Unfortunately this came to my mind at about 3 in the morning. It made me sit up in bed as I realized how stupid I've been not to think of it sooner.

But who fits this description best? My eyes were now wide open in wonderment, as Sarah rolled over next to me in bed as though awakened by my squirming. I could think of only one person...Marlis-it must be Marlis!...the health advocate who appeared intent on praying for Al in his room-who came across as a living saint. After all, she had been in and out of his room often and secretly at night...and she was at that Elroy meeting.

Sarah, now as awake as I am, almost jumped out of bed when I did as I rushed to the phone to make a quick call to Chief Hermes regarding my thoughts about Marlis.

"Joe, what the heck are you doing? Are you sick or something?" Sarah asked.

"Yeah...sick of letting my uncle be exposed to all those 'sickies' who may harm him." Not taking the time to explain further, I hurriedly dialed the chief's home phone number.

Expecting to hear the wrath of the chief for bothering him so early in the morning, I ignored the consequences and hung onto the receiver even though the ringing kept going on and on. When someone did answer it must have been his wife. She couldn't understand me at first, but when I mentioned my name she quickly called her husband to the phone.

"Joe, what the hell are you doing man. Do you know what time it is?"

"Yeah…it's early. But I can't sleep thinking about my uncle. For one thing, he no longer has a guard at his room. The DEA guard is a suspect. Al needs one desperately. I have a hunch who might do him harm. Can you please get a police guard stationed at his door…now?"

"Calm down. Sure I can do that. I know how you must feel after hearing about your uncle. Whoever it is, we'll be certain not to let them enter," assured the chief. I noted, "But it could be anyone chief., so be extra careful who's entering the room…at least for the next few days. The only exceptions should be me and doctor Hamid Lahn, who can enter at anytime, plus only those attendants cleared by DEA and fully authorized by hospital administration."

I realize there's surveillance devices in the room, but I also remember that none of these worked too well…neither the cameras nor the special two-way mirrors. Perhaps they were tampered with, or an "insider" knew where they are. In any case, I was quick to warn the chief how urgent it is to keep this confidential and that if Lahn gets to the room to let me know immediately…hoping, of course, that he'll show up soon.

To soften the blow of having him assign a police officer to such a task at this time of the morning, I assured the chief that it probably won't be long before the room can be left unguarded—realizing, of course, that Al may be a vegetable soon (or hopefully well enough to be removed to another room that's more secure).

The chief agreed, but after pausing briefly he coughed as though this gave him more time to consider what he was hearing, and said…"Joe, are you also safe? Sounds like you may need some protection, if all these sinister people get wind of what you know you could be their next victim."

His warning took me by surprise. All this time I wasn't thinking that the information I was gathering could alert the evil doers into also trying to shut me up.

"Just watch your back, Joe. I've been in this business long enough to know that they'll even try to take a cop out if they think he's onto them."

"Well, I always have my pistol loaded...if that's any comfort. But I don't think they're dumb enough to shoot a cop considering the consequences."

"Don't be too sure. There are all kinds of ways they can get you, even poison or induced drug overdose—perhaps how your uncle got into his condition. You're dealing with some pretty smart and clever people. Are you sure you don't want a partner with you? I could assign one easy enough."

"Dunno—about the only one I might need would be Charley McKay our narcotic dick. He seemed aware of such kingpins like Frankie Natole and knows how some of these druggies think and behave. Plus he's easy and trustworthy to have around."

"You got him. I recall you two work well together. I'll take Charley off his present duties and have him available for you tomorrow. It'll take me a while to go over all this with him."

I felt relieved and more secure knowing that McKay will be my backup. He helped me round up those drug terrorists at our giant shopping mall, and before that assisted me with capturing the notorious leader of that gang of suspects often meeting at a phony fitness club in a Twin Cities suburb.

This also means with McKay's backup I can devote more time to finding doctor Lahn, who warned that unless Al is quickly and properly helped he will die or suffer not only serious brain damage but also even possible nerve damage, memory loss, and maybe even lose some use of his hands and arms. Knowing Al, he'd prefer dying rather than go through all this.

But hopefully he'll be able to survive for at least the next two days and receive fast help from comatose expert doctor Lahn. After all, things aren't all bad. Fortunately, in the latest report I received, Al's feeding tubes are still working as well as all the other vital connections keeping him alive.

On my way out the door, Sarah reminded me that the weather outside is so cold I need an extra warm coat. Winter really came on fast, but after all this is Minnesota and I should be ready for it. Thinking of that, I put the coat on over a bullet-proof vest and checked my gun.

I learned from experience it's always wise to make sure my gun is loaded. Also, I kept the chief's words in mind: "watch your back!."

But what was going on behind my back involving my uncle is almost impossible to figure out. I only know that Elroy has obviously put together a variety of characters to do his bidding, from thugs to respected community and health care leaders.

It's now mostly up to me and Charley to weed out the bad from the good. The trouble is, this could take some time—and Al has hardly any left.

I was reminded, however, upon returning to my desk, that I also have help from my DEA contact Terry Johnson. He left a message for me to call him and labeled it urgent. In my mind, everything now seems to be urgent. I chose to call Terry first before taking time to welcome McKay as my partner, thinking Johnson may at last have some good news regarding finding Lahn.

But, alas, this wasn't to be. Instead, Terry told me Lahn now seems to have disappeared from the face of the earth. But he's still searching for him and has contacted nearly everyone who knows Lahn, including his clinic contacts, to get some leads as to his whereabouts. So far, though, the leads have led no where.

"How about Sylvia?—his beloved niece, she may have an idea where he is."

"We've already asked her—but either she's afraid to say or she sincerely doesn't know," Terry explained.

"Are there any leads at all who McKay can also check out? He's so darn familiar with 'who's who' in narcotics around here that he should be able to help locate him."

"It's like playing checkers, Joe. The guy with all the kings is Elroy, and we're just trying to get him in a corner to keep him from doing more harm. If we have too many of our opponents around he can jump us more easily and before you know he has all our chips."

"But you needn't worry about McKay. He works well behind the scenes. There's probably no one outside of the precinct who would know he's working on this. He's always been rather shy of publicity and even his wife probably doesn't know for sure what he does."

I added, "In this case, let's have him go directly to the top—Elroy himself—to see what we can get on him to flush him out and tell us where Lahn is."

"We already have a lot on him, thanks to your uncle's notes. But it may be smarter to have Charley pretend to be a disgruntled cop who could be bribed by Elroy to keep updated on your activities," Terry suggested.

"Hmn...I think we can put that together, Terry. I'll clue in the chief and others here."

"The fewer to know the better," my DEA pal urged. "Hopefully Charley can put on an act that'll make everyone believe—except for you or me and perhaps the chief—that he's fed up with the police department. At least enough that Elroy will confide in him."

"Good point!—maybe it can be because he's being made my partner...and he doesn't want this. For that matter, it is about time Charley is promoted to at least a captain."

There was some unexplained pause...it lasted for more than a few minutes. Did Terry drop the phone, or something? "Hello, hello—are you still there pal?" I asked, wondering why he suddenly stopped talking.

"Yeah...I was just thinking about that excuse for McKay's joining up with Elroy. I don't think that'll work, Joe. It sounds kinda phony. If Elroy gets suspicious at all, this whole plan could backfire...also it could put Charley in danger. On second thought, I believe we have a better chance by using a detective who has nothing at all to do with drugs...like some rookie cop who is disappointed with the force and wants a job as a security man for politicians."

I had to agree...this way there's no direct connection with me nor narcotics. The guy seems rather normal in this day and age...a young man with ambition trying to find a job he likes more and probably pays more. At the same time, someone who can be trusted to be an undercover for us so we can more effectively nab Elroy...and, of course, help protect me from maybe getting killed-which is especially appealing to me.

But who can fill that role? The best person to tell me that, of course, would be the chief. I hope he hasn't already gotten to McKay about partnering with me.

Unfortunately, as I approached the chief's office I could notice the chief and Charley already meeting. The large window surrounding his door enabled them to be observed in silhouette form as the chief moved his arms and Charley crossed his. Whatever the discussion, it seemed rather dramatic.

The chief's secretary buzzed his office when I asked to see him and I could notice the chief walking quickly to open the door as Charley waited for me to arrive. They apparently knew why I was coming and were well prepared.

"Joe, we've talking about your uncle's situation and the need for your extra security."

"Yeah, and about that S.O.B. Elroy," added McKay.

Before they could continue, I quickly shared with them my recent conversation with Terry and his concern that someone not associated with drug-busting be selected to be my partner to avoid Elroy from becoming suspicious. Hopefully, there could be someone in our department who could pass off as a type of young intern who wants a different type job...namely a bodyguard or security guy. They didn't interrupt, but nodded apparently in agreement as I related the DEA concerns. I was pleased to hear their response after I finished.

"Makes sense," said the chief..."I agree," concurred McKay. However, the chief added, "I'm not sure we have exactly that type of guy you describe. God knows, we have interns coming and going around here, but the person we need for this should be especially trustworthy and not be afraid to face danger."

"And be able to inform us well enough so we can finally get the goods on Elroy," emphasized McKay.

"Also also don't forget, Joe, he must be a straight shooter himself and be able to adequately protect you if necessary," cautioned the chief.

But they're both missing the most important requirement, which is why I said: "And above all, that he can help find out where doctor Lahn is so the doctor can rush to the hospital and help my uncle snap out of his coma."

"Anyone fit that description?" I asked, noticing the sudden quiet.

"Maybe…there's one new guy here who seems determined to be the best damn cop in the world. He's always asking how he can improve and is interested in knowing all about our procedures and guidelines." the chief said snapping his fingers.

"Let me guess…you don't mean George Owens?" McKay asked.

"That's the guy. He also has a knack at asking questions and being able to interrogate smoothly with good results. He'd be able to find out where Frenole is without anyone becoming suspicious and has a way of making others think he's sincerely interested in them. Plus, he appears to be a brave and sensible fellow willing to take on risky assignments."

"In other words, he'd make a good coverup investigator," McKay summed up.

"And I'm sure he'd be accepted by Elroy to inform him of what we might know about the councilman and his underworld. Also, hopefully we can be assured that he'll help lead them all to prison," remarked the chief smiling.

Assured that Owens will accept this covert role, I breathed a little easier and anxiously awaited the time when the chief and McKay will ask me to meet with Owens to further describe his new duties. We all knew that timing is crucial.

One thing for certain, I'll let Owens know the most important thing to do is find out where doctor Lahn might be, I thought glancing at my watch ticking away the time when Al would be facing a deadly crisis. My God, there's only a little more than a day left before that happens. Just then my cell phone jingled. The code name TJ came up again so I knew the caller. I also noticed my hand was trembling when answering the call as I wondered if Terry now has any good news to report about the status of the two doctors…hopefully that Frenole has given him more information about where the hell Lahn may be.

"Again, Joe, no news is good news," were Terry's first words. "However, although we haven't found Lahn yet we think we're getting very close…but we also know how close you're uncle is running out of time. So if you have any more clues as to how to bring Lahn to your uncle as fast as possible please keep me posted. Frenole still refuses to tell us anything."

This, of course, at least gave me a chance to inform him about George Owens being assigned by the chief to spy on Elroy by joining up with him and his crooked pals in hope he can get some information that could provide some answers to all this…and also get more substantial evidence about Elroy's illegal drug activities. I knew, however, Terry wouldn't click off before commenting that we may be interfering with his DEA's efforts…and he did just that. But I also realized that whatever means we can use at this point is okay as long as we end this suspense-filled drama as quickly and as successfully as possible.

All this time, though, my gut feeling is to go face-to-face with that s.o.b. Elroy. I even felt this way driving home from work in my own car rather than the squad wondering how he'd react being attacked and walloped to confess to his drug dealing. Who knows…some punches to the jaw might help clear his memory.

In fact, I had the urge to turn my car around in the middle of the freeway and head back to where Elroy does his politicking in hope of finding and working him over 'till he tells me what he's done with Lahn, and above all…what he's done to Al. I can imagine him smirking over all this—.and only hope George Owens can wipe that off Elroy's face.

My car must have spun a little too much when I was deciding whether to turn back to punch Elroy in the chop. The driver behind me honked his horn and then tried to nudge me over to the side of the road. Luckily, I knew a few police tricks and avoided tipping over. I was amazed how bold this driver was. Instead of slowing down he now kept bumping my car and motioning for me to pull over and stop.

God, that's about all I need…an enraged driver. Since I was driving my own car I had nothing on it to indicate I was a cop. Upset by all this, but knowing not to get involved with rage-driving, I continued on until the guy drove ahead of me and began applying his brakes on and off to interrupt my driving.

That did it! My anger gave way to parking on a safe spot off the road to chew this guy out for reckless driving. He also parked, flung open his door and rushed toward me. I kept thinking is he crazy? What's he going to do? All the time, feeling the pistol on my belt just in case I need it.

The guy's young and wanting a fight. He hollered,"What the hell you trying to do…are you drunk? You nearly turned into my car—you dumb ass." I began apologizing but he refused to hear it. What startled me most was what he was holding. It looked like a tire wrench. He wanted to know my name and address, and then tried to open my car door…that's when I reached for my gun. On seeing that, he drew back and began returning to his car. It was like this whole event was staged. Fortunately, I got his license plate number as he drove off.

Whew! I continued heading home still shook over what took place and wondering what the hell that was all about. However, I thought it would be just a matter of phoning my precinct to see who belongs to that car. I only had to wait a few moments before our information desk reported that it was an official vehicle belonging to the state, and the driver could be any licensed state employee. But since when did all state workers start carrying guns? Although concealed weapons are now allowed in the state by those authorized, this guy seemed very unauthorized and apparently wanted me to see a pistol inside his coat as he held that wrench.

Shortly after arriving home I told my wife about my road-rage experience and then called Terry to inform him. He responded calmly, offering a reason for this scary experience.

"It's possible that Elroy wants to discredit you…before you can do it to him. He probably sent his hired gun out to either blow you away or get you in a spot where you can be reported as being a delinquent driver…perhaps with too much to drink.

"I'll bet we read about this soon in the local media. It seems like Elroy's already onto our suspicions of him and what's happening. The fact that he's trying to keep you from investigating him makes me believe he'd probably do anything to make the public regard you as someone you can't believe."

"In other words, when the accusations are coming in about Elroy's criminal activities he'll be able to counteract by pointing to my faults and failures instead?"

"Exactly, and this in turn will take some of the negative accusations off of him. These politicians, Joe…they can be extremely clever."

"Yeah, I can just see the headline: 'Twin Cities Cop Found Drunk; Unable to Drive Properly.'"

Terry added, "and the subtitle might be: "Detective Called A Risk for Other Drivers on Busy Freeway." This thought bothered me most as I tried relaxing at home.

I hastily ate the delicious dinner cooked up by Sarah, interrupted by constantly checking my watch to see how much time Al has left according to the missing doctor Lahn.

"Where the hell is Lahn…what did they do to him? If he's dead, so is Al," I mumbled with almost every bite of food. Even my toddler and the dog backed away from me sensing I was much too serious to play games with them.

This unusual quiet around the dinner table was suddenly broken when Sarah asked, "Do you suppose Lahn is in cahoots with those bad guys?"

"Who knows…there's just so many of those types out there, some may have bought him out. I just hope our inside man, Owens, can supply me with some fast answers."

It was as though the good lord heard my plea. Before I even wiped my face and drank the last drop of coffee in my cup, the phone in the kitchen rang loud and clear.

Sarah beat me to it. She was expecting a call from her mother regarding a social event in the neighborhood to meet some new residents. All I could do was tap my fingers on the table and nervously check my watch as she and her mom chatted.

Knowing this could take a long time, I was very surprised when Sarah hung up so soon. She loudly announced, "Joe, someone's been trying to call us. There's something on our caller ID."

Grabbing the phone I joined Sarah looking for the caller. However, no name came up on our call directory other than the word "anonymous."

But fortunately, the phone number also was listed. Neither Sarah nor I had the slightest idea who wanted to reach us, but we both shrugged it off as just another telemarketer—...even though we left word in the prescribed manner for none to call us. If they did, this was now a violation of a state law. So we ignored this until my curiosity prompted me to check out the phone number. I clicked onto it—expecting someone to answer selling something or making a pitch for a phony cause. In fact, I had my reply all ready—namely if they continue calling I'll report them to the attorney general. But the voice that answered surprisingly sounded vaguely familiar.

"Mr. Kavinsky—this is George Owens." I could barely hear him as though he's whispering. "I'm calling from a phone I use for my undercover work. I thought it best to update you on what I've found out at the Elroy office so far."

"And?"—I asked anxiously, impressed by this conscientious and very aggressive young guy eager to prove himself as a competent member of our detective organization.

He responded, "And I've learned that...yes—Elroy has pegged you as an obstacle in his way to the mayor's job. He's assigned some of his group to block you from investigating his plans and, frankly, I'd be very careful if I were you. It wasn't too difficult to be accepted into his organization but I think I should get an Oscar for pretending how much I dislike working for the chief. He seemed to fall for this hook, line and sinker."

I again warned, "Hopefully George—but you can't be too sure of a person like Elroy. Make certain you don't do anything that'll cause him to become suspicious. Chances are they'll be watching your every move and asking you all kinds of questions about the police department. And I'm glad you know our secret phone system.

"And by the way…what does he have you doing for him?"

"So far, just sort of running errands. I'm to make sure the media gets his latest news and arrange photo-ops for him, as well as travel with some of his henchmen"

"I think I've already met one of them. He accosted me on the freeway and accused me of driving drunk. My guess is that they'll try to convince the press to do a story on this—making me look pretty bad and hard for readers to believe if, and when, I tell them about Elroy's drug operations."

But I again emphasized my primary interest is learning the whereabouts of doctor Lahn. However, at this time Owens hadn't heard anything about him. He knew my concern but said Lahn hasn't been mentioned at all, at least not in his presence. With a promise that he'd make this top priority, Owens suddenly said he had to click off talking with me.

Having some experience in undercover work myself, I know it's sometimes risky being seen even talking quietly on a cell phone. So Owens' abrupt exit from the phone wasn't too unexpected. Anyway, I now know how to contact him.

To take my mind off such serious subjects, I challenged my wife to a game of Dominoes at home, and even let Maddie get involved. Sarah likes this game, playing it often when company comes, and switching over to Bridge when her card club gets together. She loves a challenge and, as she notes, this is also good for the mind…especially to keep the memory sharp.

However, at this time such conversation about mind and memory made me think all the more of Al and how close he is to losing both. Poor Al, he loved playing Dominoes, too.

I was finally winning this silly game when our kitchen wall phone interrupted. It rang enough times that neither Sarah nor I thought we could get to it fast enough from our living room table where the game was being played. In fact, I nearly stumbled over Stella the dog as Maddie giggled as though we're suddenly playing tag…her favorite game.

"It's for you," whispered Sarah almost out of breath. She touched a finger to her lips indicating that I should be quiet as she whispered—"It's some guy who calls himself doctor."

I grabbed the phone, almost pushing Sarah away from it, eagerly hoping it was doctor Lahn. But even when I pressed my ear to the receiver about all I could hear was rather heavy breathing. Whoever it was seemed awfully out of breath.

In between breaths I could barely make out that it was indeed from Lahn. "Mr. Kavinsky, I can't talk long to you…I just escaped Frenole and his gang. I'm now hiding in a corner of an alley and using my cell phone which I concealed in my underwear. It was difficult for me to elude them, but once I had the chance I ran as fast as possible."

Trying to calm him down a little, I asked, "Where are you now?…Is there a way I can rescue you?"

"I'm afraid not. It's best that I keep as far away from them as possible. I'm not familiar with this end of the city but have noticed there are lots of cabs and buses going by."

He continued, "Keep in mind I have not forgotten your uncle nor his declining condition. I realize we only have a very short time left to help him."

"Can you get to him now?...take a cab or whatever you can get. You know where his hospital is at I hope. You've been there before."

"Yes, the most important reason I'm calling you, in fact, is to let you know I plan to see your uncle as fast as I can. I hope this can be done in a few minutes by taking a cab. Can I get into his room or is it guarded?"

"There's supposed to be a guard at the door, but he knows if you come to let you in. I gave him your name. Hopefully Frenole hasn't taken away any of your credentials."

"No, but I fear he'll be after me as soon as they realize I'm missing. I hope your guard will keep them out since I need some time to treat your uncle and do all I can to bring him through this nightmare."

"I want to be with you...I'll try leaving now and it should only take me about fifteen minutes to get there. Believe me doctor Lahn there won't be anyone interfering with you when I'm in the room."

"Fine, but even if you're late I'll start assisting him. Time is most critical."

He needn't tell me that, for the last few days I've been checking my watch and almost noticing every second that flies by. When I heard him click off, I nearly spilled the dominoes all over the floor as I jumped up and raced for my car keys. All I could mutter to my startled wife and child was "Gotta go...have to rush to the hospital for Al."

Sarah had the door opened and my car keys in hand as I raced out of the house. I could hear her say "good luck" while I headed for my car. I seldom use the squad car except for official emergencies...but I cursed to myself for not having it this time in my driveway cause this was perhaps he biggest emergency I've had to face since joining the force.

My foot was heavy on the gas pedal as I passed many slow-moving vehicles on the freeway, thinking only of getting to Al's room on time to be with doctor Lahn. Exceeding the speed limit wasn't in my mind at all when I observed a car that appeared to be tailing me most of the way.

I wasn't too concerned at first...that is until the guy behind the wheel began flashing his lights on and off and hollering out his window for me to pull over. Since he also had a portable light twirling on top of his car, similar to those used on unmarked highway patrol cars, I heeded his warning and angrily drove to a safe place off the road and parked as demanded.

As he got out of his car, though, he wasn't in a highway patrol uniform but did have a small badge on his shirt. All I could think was, "God why now?...how can I get out of this fast?

As he slowly walked over to my car he began to look very familiar. Damn, he seems to be the same guy who was involved in the road rage I experienced. I wasn't sure, however, until he came closer after checking my license plate with a flashlight.

Although he pulled his cap down to somewhat hide his face, I could still tell that this was indeed the jerk who almost ran me down when I tried turning my car on a road when I was thinking about going back to face Elroy man to man. At that time, however, I had a gun...this time I left the gun at home in my rush to get to the hospital.

He talked gruffly, almost faking his voice, as he focused the flashlight on my face.

"Where you going pal? Do you know you're speeding. Let's see your license."

"The name's Joe Kavinsky…I'm a police officer and in an emergency situation which is why I'm in such a hurry."

"I don't give a damn who you are. When you violate the speed law it's my duty to stop you, he said looking over my license. I'll have to give you a ticket and since we don't take money or credit cards you'll have to follow me to the highway patrol station."

"Where the hell is that?" I asked staring at him in almost disbelief over his haughty and belligerent manner.

"I'll show you…follow my car! There's a shortcut to the station through that cornfield next to us."

"Are you crazy? You're the one interfering with police work fella. I'm going nowhere with you. Now get out of my way so I can get on with my duties."

With that the obnoxious guy put his hand on his pistol. About the only thing I could do was to follow my police academy training when a situation like this occurs…With all my strength I pushed against my door and forced him backward. Fortunately, I caught him by surprise…enough to seize his gun hand and hit him as hard as possible in the belly.

He doubled up, enabling me to push him to the ground and hold his arms down. He was still fighting me to the point where I thought he'd kill me if he could. But I was able to seize his gun and pointed it right at him, which caused him finally to give up.

"You bastard, you're the same idiot that stopped me on the freeway earlier today aren't you. What the hell is your game?…you're not from the highway patrol…If there's any arrest made I'll be doing it. I may have forgotten my gun, but not my cuffs".

With my grasp on his gun, which I poked in his face, I was able to turn him over and slap the cuffs on him despite his cursing and struggle to get up. "This is how the police arrest hoodlums buddy," I hollered back at him. But now what am I going to do with him?

Luckily, I did take my cell phone with me. It was also lucky I was able to catch Charley McKay still working at the precinct. While holding the creep down and talking to McKay on my cell phone, I explained to him my situation and asked him to please rush to where all this is happening and help bring this guy to the station so I can continue rushing to my uncle's bedside.

Knowing the Twin Cities like the palm of his hand, Charley assured me he's on the way. It seemed like forever though before I saw him racing down the road. I spent most of the time before that just pointing my pistol at the guy still on the ground and trying to find out why he was pursuing me.

He was scowling all the time and refused to talk. The only time he seemed to respond at all was when Charley drove up.

"Don't I know you?" were the first words out of McKay's mouth when he glanced at the jerk who apparently wanted to either kill me outright…or do so on the way to a make-believe highway patrol station.

"You're another one of Frankie Frenole's gang aren't you?" declared McKay, who knows nearly every member of that group because of his longtime duties as a narcotics investigator. "I've seen you around town and know you're on probation for drug dealing. I also know you have some contacts with the big shots who offer you contract work."

"What kind of contract work?" I asked naïvely.

"Joe—for God's sake this guy's a hit man. I've been trying to put him behind bars for a long time."

"Well, he's also quite an actor. He almost had me fooled into thinking he was some sort of highway patrol officer."

Charley, looked at me rather puzzled and waived his hands, "Joe, listen up for God's sake—I said he's a contract killer…he works for others who pay him to kill."

Now squirming to get up, the guy on the ground could only curse and even tried spitting on us when we looked closer at his ugly face…That's when I finally lost patience and grabbed him by the throat. I then noticed his big collar, and grabbed onto it to help me bring him back on his feet.

"You son of a bitch, who hired you? Why are you getting in my face. We want an answer, and we want it now."

"Easy Joe," cautioned Charley. "We'll question him at the police station."

"You'd better hurry…Al may be dying because of such punks." I warned.

"If we know who's behind this, Charley, I'll be able to deal more effectively and maybe have a better chance to help Al."

"I know you're in a big hurry to do that, Joe, so why don't you continue heading on to the hospital while I take this hoodlum back to the precinct. I'll call you on your cell when we find out anything…okay?"

I jumped back into my car and once again pressed down hard on the accelerator to resume my fast trip to the hospital...where Al may be gasping his last breath.

But my cell phone interfered once again with my glum thoughts, however. It blared almost louder than the roar of my overheated engine. I knew it couldn't be McKay already, and it wasn't. Instead it was the gentle but unusually nervous voice of my wife.
Only this time she sounded as if she was about to cry.

"Joe, it's aunt Kay...something's happened to her."

"What do you mean—happened to her"?

"She's disappeared. I was talking with her on the phone after you left. She screamed, saying there's a man in the house and hung up. I called her neighbor right away who checked the house but said Kay wasn't there but everything in it is scattered about."

Trying to calm Sarah down somewhat, I rationalized that perhaps Kay knew the man and they left the house for some good reason...like giving directions or discussing the need to paint the house...after all, it must be at least 50 years old.

But I could sense she wasn't buying any of this and felt guilty trying to mask my fear as to what really may have happened to Kay. Although my mind was filled with the need to rush to the hospital, I also began imagining all kinds of terrifying things I withheld from Sarah until she clicked off her phone.

For instance, perhaps someone found out that Al had drafts of his story on Elroy tucked away in his house. I wiped my brow thinking of that, and how lucky it was we obtained so many stories he was working on—but, unfortunately not enough. If anyone did know besides my aunt, wife, and me then that person must have had a special inside source.

The more I thought about this, the more I ruled out such close acquaintances as Al's editor who seemed very 'tight-lipped' about mentioning the drafts to anyone but me; my very reliable DEA pal Johnson, and, of course, Kay and Sarah. However, knowing human nature, it may be possible that my old aunt could have innocently talked about this to a neighbor over the backyard fence, or for that matter Terry may have mentioned it to some trusty agent over coffee…after all, Terry's former guard at Al's door betrayed him. All this, of course, could have been done with the best intentions, but like the old slogan used during our war with Hitler: "A Slip of The Lip Can Sink A Ship."

But what could I do enclosed in a car on the way to make sure my uncle was receiving help? I desperately thought about who to call…someone who could back me up while I'm confined in my out-of-date, and nearly out of gas, car on such a mercy mission.

I didn't want to bother Johnson again who's already busy checking out all those suspects I listed for him. And McKay is already interrogating that guy who just about killed me on the highway. About the only one I really haven't asked for assistance from is chief Hermes, who also knows Al as well as that s.o.b. Elroy and what he may be plotting.

But my call to the chief was frustrating. No one answered, not even Liz our secretary. I was about to click off when I finally heard the chief on the phone as if he had been running to get it. His monitor showed who was calling. "Joe, McKay phoned, said he's bringing in someone who tried knocking you off the road. What the hell's that all about?"

I explained as quickly as possible, while still steering around some road work enroute to the hospital. I focused mainly on Kay's disappearance and the need for some cops to check out where the hell my dear elderly aunt might be. "From all appearances, she may have been harmed by someone who broke into her home, chief."

It was a big relief to talk to the chief since he's quick to take action. And I'm glad, too, that he was beginning to lose respect for Elroy. Like me, he was growing more suspicious about the councilman every day. He no longer seemed hesitant to criticize him.

For that matter, I'm certain the chief would never want to report to Elroy—even if he won the mayoral election and became the chief's boss. That became even more obvious when I suggested that Elroy may be involved in trying to thwart my attempts to help Al, who apparently was all set to expose this guy for what he is.

"I'll keep all this in mind, Joe, while we put out an all-points bulletin to find your aunt. You'll be the first to know when we get any information…and please make sure you let me know the progress you're making to save your uncle."

Progress was the wrong word. About every mile or so I was either running into a detour or a long line of traffic congestion. I fully understand why Minnesota is described as having two seasons…winter and road construction.

But going bumper-bumper gave me lots of time to think about my best strategy upon arriving at the hospital. I knew the guard at the door was commanded not to allow anyone into Al's room unless it's doctor Lahn. So, I had to convince the guard of my credentials. The slow-moving traffic also gave me some extra time to search through my pockets and wallet to find anything further to substantiate my being permitted to enter—besides police ID.

I quickly began looking for my DEA credential—a laminated card covered and labeled "family facts" to conceal it The card was deep in my wallet to also discourage anyone searching for it Removing it from the cover was tough, as intended, but finally—there it was.

I couldn't help but think how properly hidden this card is…hell, it's indeed a helpful coverup without disclosing I'm also a federal undercover investigator. Moreover, it gives me some extra confidence to charge ahead and conquer obstacles in the way of seeing Al.

The obstacles occured in numerous ways, in addition to detours and traffic jams. I didn't have my cell phone handy when it started to jingle again. But I shoved it too far from me while rummaging through my wallet and couldn't reach it. Luckily, I had to stop for a road sign but was unable to grab the phone before the jingling stopped. The caller left a message.

"Joe, it's me Charley. I'm calling from a phone in our interrogation area. Just wanted you to know that—yes…that road rage guy works for Elroy. He was asked to whack you and get you out of the way. We're still questioning him but thought you should know this before getting to the hospital. Also, if you need me there just let me know on your cell."

I wasn't too surprised…after all Terry and others cautioned me that I might be a target by knowing too much. At least one of my risks has been eliminated by knowing that the rage guy will now be locked up. Whoever else is out to get me…God only knows.

I also finally had a straight and clear way to the hospital when my damn cell phone jingled again. Only this time the phone was very close to me. I thought at first, however, that the phone's battery was wearing out…I could barely hear the person who was trying to tell me something in a very urgent way.

Chapter 26

▼

"Mr. Kavinsky, it is I—doctor Lahn. I'm with your uncle. The guard let me in." Immediately recognizing the voice of doctor Lahn, who always introduces himself in this manner, I replied "Great! How are you doing? And above all, how's my uncle?"

"He still appears deep in sleep, but I have brought with me many items and techniques I believe will resuscitate him. Although struggling, he seems determined to escape from this terrible coma."

This relieved much of the tension I was feeling during my almost hectic bumper-to-bumper car ride on the freeway. Although swerving quickly to avoid hitting a huge truck trying to pass me, I was able to respond, "I'm on my way and should be there in a few more minutes."

But there's no response from him. "Doctor Lahn...doctor Lahn—do you hear me? I'm almost at the hospital." Still silence. In hope of regaining his attention, I spoke louder this time, almost yelling: "Please answer...do you hear me now?"

Thinking the problem may be my cell phone, I began tapping it with my finger and striking it on the side hoping to get an answer. Still nothing. There was no sign of the battery needing recharging. However, I thought for a moment I heard some talking in the background. After yelling for a response again, I gave up and nearly tossed the damn phone.

Oh great…now there's two more people I need to worry about—doc Lahn who may have been assaulted in Al's room and my aunt who may have been kidnapped.

All this made me accelerate more. I was only minutes away now from the ramp turnoff to the hospital. I glanced once more at my watch to see how many minutes I had left before Lahn predicted my uncle would probably be a vegetable. My God…there was only a half-hour remaining.

I couldn't find a regular parking spot when I arrived in the crowded ramp and spent at least another ten minutes searching for a nearby handicap parking site. After squeezing into one, almost scraping the side of my car, I had trouble squeezing out of my car door, which was nearly against the car next to me with a handicap card dangling on the inside front window. Unfortunately, I didn't have such a sign and almost felt like stealing it if I could.

Ignoring the risk of being fined $200 for illegal parking in a handicap zone, I finally freed myself from my car and, after being tempted a little about trying to open the door of that car next to me to see if I could seize his handicap sign, ran to the entrance of the hospital.

Rushing up the hospital stairs, I fled by the reception counter…probably leaving the attendants behind it wondering what the hell my big hurry was all about. Fortunately, since I've been in this hospital before, I knew where to find the elevator going to Al's floor.

But before entering the elevator, I looked around to see if Charley McKay was anywhere in sight. I recalled he would try to get here to assist me if I needed any help. But he was nowhere in sight, so maybe he was still questioning that rage guy…or maybe he beat me to Al's room, or dodged the detours since he was coming from another direction.

Deep in thought as to what I'll find when I get there, I was startled when a very large guy got in my way when the elevator doors opened. He was reading a newspaper and apparently didn't notice me racing to the elevator before the doors closed. The collision with him almost knocked me over. But I was upset even more by the fact that he didn't even apologize.

The newspaper still covered most of his face as he continued reading it. I tried hard to ignore him but something about this fella seemed sort of strange. Stepping back into the elevator to allow him plenty of room, I nearly bumped into another guy. He seemed sort of familiar for some reason and also was reading a paper that covered his face. He didn't say anything, but simply moved to the back of the elevator, almost squeezing me into a corner.

I noticed the button was already pushed to the floor I wanted, so I was surprised when it stopped enroute. But I knew why…I saw the big guy put his newspaper down and deliberately push the stop button. At this time, I became upset realizing seconds were ticking away to get to my uncle. I couldn't help but say, "Hey, what's the matter? Don't slow this elevator down pal…I'm in a very big hurry to get to a patient's room."

"Shut your damn mouth!…We're here to make certain you don't."

I almost froze hearing those words. My first reaction was to reach for my gun, but I wasn't fast enough. The guy with me in the corner already was holding a gun.

But his gun wasn't pointing at me…it was directed at the head of the big guy who suddenly looked startled. "What the hell you doing?…you're one of us," he yelled.

What the hell's happening? Was all I could think. My answer came when the fella in my corner looked at me as he kept his gun on the big guy. In fact, he actually smiled a little.

My lord…it's George Owens, the guy the chief assigned to be an undercover to spy on councilman Elroy. No wonder he looked familiar. I didn't know what to say at the moment but knew I should help George keep the would-be attacker under control.

The big guy threw a punch at Owens almost knocking the gun from his hands. I could see it bloodied George's nose as he backed away. In turn I jumped in and threw some punches at the face of the attacker, with one landing hard on the guy's chin. When he toppled a little I threw another as hard as possible into his large stomach, causing him to double up.

That's all George and I needed…we both pounced on him and, while holding his gun hand against the floor, resumed hitting him in the face until he apparently was unconscious.

"That's enough, George," I warned as the attacker groaned and laid still.

Owens explained, "It was a setup, Joe. I heard about their plans as I was snooping around. The Elroy group said to stop you anyway possible from getting to your uncle. I tried warning you sooner but couldn't contact you in time."

"Yeah…I was too busy on the freeway. But that's another story…I'm sure glad you were there when I needed you."

"I thought it best to disguise myself and be on that elevator when this guy spots you entering it. He agreed to have me involved since he knew you're a cop and that there may be some gun-play," noted Owens.

When we finally reached Al's floor I left the attacker with George and made a beeline to my uncle's room, still hoping for the best. I realized, however, that Owens' cover was gone by this incident which would alert Elroy that we're on to him. As I ran to the room, I could still hear George lugging the gunman out of the elevator.

Approaching the room I no longer saw a guard at the door. Did someone also get rid of him? and what will I find when I enter...will Lahn still be there? These and many other questions filled my mind as I raced to get some answers—so far there's none I could really understand. What's happening? *Why* am I running into such terrible unforeseen problems?

* * * *

Al was also grasping for answers at this time as his so-called nightmare became even worse. He not only was still gasping for air from the struggle he so vividly recalled to smother him in bed, but was now trying to climb up that awesome tunnel he fell into after meeting some people he knew who had died years ago. Everything around him was now almost pitch black and his shouts were in vain. He couldn't see anyone to help him.

Being a good Christian all his life, he began praying but realized that he couldn't concentrate on anything other than making sure his tired feet and clutching hands continued to move him upward.

His goal, at least at this critical time, was mainly to see some flicker of light from above, indicating there was some way out of this hell hole. At this time he no longer wanted to reach the light at the bottom.

He longed for the open arms of his beloved wife and his loyal nephew Joe. At times he imagined Kay was beckoning to him while Joe yelled encouragement to keep climbing. But he feared that, like a mirage in the desert, they would quickly disappear and perhaps vanish forever. He tried shouting: "I'm coming!...I'm coming!" but this made him more fatigued. He knew, however, that he can never give up and that if he even paused to catch his breath he could topple backward once more into that black and eerie end of the tunnel seemingly waiting to smother him. He was almost breathless...like his nephew was at this very moment.

But Al could feel his heart beginning to beat stronger, although his breathing still came in gasps as he climbed higher despite exhaustion. In fact, he was almost ready to give up when he saw a tiny beam of light ahead. His hope was somewhat restored by the light from above, thinking he might...just might...be able to save himself if he can only continue to move upward.

In desperation, he forced himself to go further up and began shouting for help as he got closer to the light. But he realized there may not be anyone up there to hear him. Or was there? For a moment he thought he heard someone talking. Could it be that help may be awaiting him after all?

He tried going faster to find out... but he seemed to slip every time he quickened his progress. The mere thought, however, that there may indeed be someone at the top of the tunnel encouraged him to attempt to speed up even more.

But he moved his legs so fast that they slipped and he lost his balance. His grasp loosened and finally gave way causing his body to descend suddenly. There wasn't anything he could do but grit his teeth and prepare to fall into the deepest depths of terror but the voice he heard from above began to grow louder encouraging him to "hang on."

Inspired by all this, Al regained his desire, strength and determination to reach the tunnel top.

Chapter 27

I was nearly out of breath from running to my uncle's unguarded room—but was greatly relieved when I found doctor Lahn bending over him when I finally got to his bedside. The doctor was talking softly to Al…gently asking him to wake up.

"My God, is that all you can do?…I thought you had some special treatment for this," I spoke impatiently to Lahn.

The doctor raised his hand, indicating I should be quiet. "There's no magic potion for this Mr. Kavinsky…nor will there probably ever be."

But he continued with a smile, "The treatment and medication I've already given him in your absence I am pleased to report is working. To my knowledge, the coma is stopping and he should be getting out of it very shortly."

"You mean we made it in time."

"It certainly appears that way. But he could take a turn for the worst. One never can be too sure in a case like this." I wondered, "Have you been talking to him long?"

"Yes, and also praying for him. God is the best physician I know, and when all seems lost he can regain it."

Impressed by his humility and comforted by his confident manner, I had time to look at Al's face, which seemed to be more at ease than when I saw him previously. Before, he had a grim look and his face was ashen as he seemed to be struggling for breath. Now his breathing was more relaxed and his face a more normal color.

But my next question was more serious: "Is he going to be okay mentally?"

I held my breath until Lahn answered…"I'm almost certain. Only time will tell."

"How much time?"

"As soon as he awakens…he'll either be with us or brain dead."

I figured by this response. I had enough time to see if the guard had returned. Looking about I found him silently standing in a corner gazing at the door. Wondering why I didn't spot him there earlier, he explained that he knew I was coming and thought he'd be in the way in my rush to see Al. Besides, he added, by being inside the room he could be closer to the doctor in case anyone snuck in to stop Lahn from helping him.

"Has anyone else been in?" I asked accepting the guard's explanation. "Only the cleaning lady…she wanted to mop up the room. I couldn't see anything wrong with that. I tried to keep a close eye on her until she left."

"But I gave strict orders to the DEA that no one should enter except for doctor Lahn and me," I said upset over such casual indifference.

"Did you leave the room for anything?"

"Only once…just for a few minutes to go to the bathroom."

"But there's a bathroom in this room."

"Yes, but that was the time when the cleaning lady was mopping it up so I had to find another one close by in a vacant room."

I was suddenly interrupted in my questioning of the guard by doctor Lahn who cautioned against speaking too loudly since he was trying to listen to Al's heart and monitor his breathing.

"I get the feeling that your uncle is desperately trying to come out of his coma. I've used most everything I have to induce this but it seems he gets very close then falls back in his progress. This is why I need as much silence as I can get to help him and detect how this is proceeding—and perhaps I'll also need a nurse to assist me."

After I told the guard to return to duty at the door, doctor Lahn motioned me over to the bed. I almost tip-toed there to maintain the quiet he suggested. Thinking it was about something relating to Al's health I was surprised what he disclosed in a rather hushed tone: "Mr. Kavinsky the more I checked the possible reasons for your uncle's condition the more I believe it may be the result of methamphetamine given to him."

Commonly referred to as simply "meth", I knew about this horrible drug substance since it was almost running wild around the Twin Cities area lately, causing many to be addicted—from gang members to even respected young and old. In fact, some of it's taken by executives and those in high governmental circles. According to recent statistics, meth accounted for about 50 percent of drug crime in the county.

"I don't want to upset you further Mr. Kavinsky, but I couldn't help but overhear your conversation with the guard regarding meth. While in your uncle's room I found what maybe some evidence of it hidden n the bathroom."

"Like what?" I asked, knowing a little about meth due to my work with the DEA.

"Like a variety of household products, including muriatic acid, even hydrogen peroxide and other chemicals—all of which are used to manufacturer it. This is an unusual combination—but very common for producing the drug. She may have even had a small device with her to prepare it."

"Are you saying meth may have been given to my uncle?"

"Perhaps. I believe his condition may be a result of this, as well as the morphine overdose. I can detect some of it. This could prolong your uncle's comatose."

"Did you keep any of the evidence?"

"Yes, it's in my doctor bag…I thought you might be interested."

"Damn that redhead!" I nearly yelled, starling the doctor.

"What do you mean?"…doctor Lahn asked, backing off from my sudden anger.

"That cleaning lady—it must be her. She must have been giving it to him all along to keep him from waking up and telling about Elroy."

"I'm not sure what you're saying, but it does seem that your uncle was purposely kept in a coma for so long by the combination of these substances. My God, I'm surprised it didn't kill him," Lahn said.

But why wouldn't the guard have known about this? I wondered.

In trying to figure out the answer to all this, I recalled that the first guard at the door was dismissed by Terry and that the guard I just met was the one recently assigned by him. But maybe the new guy wasn't involved—and could this guard absence have been happening for some time?

As though reading my mind, doctor Lahn said this could have been going on from the time Al was first admitted to the hospital.

"Someone kept him doped up this long—hoping that this would keep him quiet forever?" I almost shouted while clenching my fists.

"Could be…but apparently whoever it was forgot to clean up all the evidence," the doctor noted.

He added, "I'm not ruling out, however, medical errors. At last count there have been some 200,000 medical mistakes reported the past year in this nation, with about eighty percent due to such errors as use of wrong drugs and perhaps doctor neglect.

"However, I'm quite certain that in your uncle's case it was a combination of both meth and drugs—plus intended medical oversight on the part of doctor Frenole. You might say he looked the other way. After all, what Frenole did to me I have very little respect for him. He's very evil and a disgrace to us doctors. I'm glad I escaped from him."

"I'm glad you did, too, and I'm sure Al will be when he hears what you've done for him." When he mentioned evil, I immediately also thought of Elroy and all the others doing his dirty work and only hope by now Terry is making headway in rounding them all up.

Again bending further over Al, Lahn resumed using his stethoscope by moving it around Al's chest and throat. He'd stop intermittently as though he was double checking something he wanted to make extra sure what he was hearing.

"Yes, he's on the way to coming out of it," the doctor said smiling again.

"Can he hear us, or know anything at all about what we're doing?"

"He may very well be aware of something. But no one really knows, since when awakened most everything's usually very difficult to remember. There are certain things, however, the comatose patient may seem to recall.

"For instance, my talking to him and encouraging him…may help in some way. He may even be aware now of the struggle to save his life."

Looking at his watch he said, "And this is why I don't want interference with what's going on. If you leave the room it'd help me concentrate more on the revival attempts."

"Is it okay if I tell his wife and mine about this…to let them know how he's doing and to be here at his bedside when and if he wakes up?" I asked.

"Certainly, when we get to that stage. I see you have a cell phone and so do I. I'll turn mine on as soon as I reach the time when that is happening."

Giving the doctor my cell phone number, I looked down at Al, patted his shoulder—the one that wasn't operated on—for support and said farewell rather than goodbye since I didn't want to leave any room for doubt that I'll be seeing him awake soon.

Sighing over all this, I walked softly out of the room and headed for the nearest place to call Terry and my wife, but not aunt Kay who may still be missing.

Before I even got to an appropriate location to make these calls, however, my cell phone jingled—it was Terry.

"Joe, how ya doing? Thought you'd like to know we found your aunt. She's okay, but a still a bit frightened. Whoever busted into her house shoved her into his car but then let her go after talking to someone on his car phone, she said. She doesn't know who it was or the caller, but I presume it was from Elroy who didn't want her to know anything about his connection with this by having her delivered to him. The story drafts are still safe since you turned these over to Owens. But Kay said they stole your uncle's computer."

It suddenly dawned on me, "But Terry...Al may have saved all this in his computer, and for that matter on a special disc. I wonder if Elroy has this?"

"Ouch!—In that case maybe he has a complete copy which makes him more prepared to defend himself with some lame excuses. But he sure doesn't need a kidnapping rap also on his shoulders. And perhaps he may see that the guy who took Kay won't be around long to talk about this to anyone."

"Well, my aunt still has a great memory and she could help you identify him I'm sure. Besides, no one can gain access into Al's computer...he has the only password."

"Perhaps, but don't be too sure. The whole thing just doesn't add up in some ways, does it Joe? We still aren't certain who should be on top of your suspect list other than Elroy. We've hesitated to arrest anyone so far in case the whole affair is so premature that even the editor who Al promised a scoop to may have outdated and different information."

"I think we're in sync on that, Terry. However, the bad group I photographed at that meeting in the gym may include one or two newcomers. Oh, and I must tell you about some additional input I obtained while in Al's room today.

"That red-headed cleaning lady may be cooking up meth and giving it to Al. Doc Lahn told me this. Your guard let her in thinking she needed to mop up the room."

I could hear a deep sigh coming from Terry, knowing he's probably saying to himself: "Hear we go again—another guard-door fiasco."

"Terry, I believe it's happened more than once considering all the evidence left in the bathroom of Al's room. The cleaning lady should know more about this…I'm almost sure there was no one else involved since the guard said he allowed no one else to enter."

"Again, Joe, don't be too sure. Who knows…some of the others on your suspect list may have helped put the stuff together and supplied the cleaning lady with it. It wasn't necessary for them to try to enter."

"You think the health care advocate had anything to do with this at night?…or for that matter the night nurse?" I asked.

"We'll know more about that, with the help of your new input regarding meth-making in the room. My first inclination is the cleaning lady must have had someone helping with this. But we have our way of finding out especially when it concerns drugs."

"Yeah…I would think the Drug Enforcement Agency certainly would be better at this than any other organization. I was a bit disappointed, however, that your guard made exceptions on his own about who enters. I thought that message was to be very clear to him. Otherwise he seemed qualified in size and muscle to keep out the bad guys."

"Believe me, the message to the guard for security was both loud and clear from us…I'll talk to him again, as well as about that drug evidence in the bathroom. Our guard should have notified us immediately—not the doctor telling you…who I'm sure had many more important things to do in that room helping your uncle."

"I feel very comfortable with Lahn, Terry. He appears quite competent and confident of Al's outcome. I don't want to criticize your guard too much either since he also seems to know what he's doing. With the doctor in the room he wanted to be near him for added protection rather than at the door all the time. But why didn't he notice something suspicious when he used the bathroom?—which I'm sure he did like all of us humans."

"Joe, we always have a backup for our guys. The hospital security at the nurse's desk was advised to fill in for the guard if he had to relieve himself. Moreover, the doctor would have noticed the meth ingredients first. Being an expert in drug overdose he would have spotted them no matter how small. You must have arrived just after all this happened.

"But despite this, I'm still pretty sure that our guard just assumed the cleaning lady was a normal necessity in every room and let her enter. He probably saw her mopping the floors and figured she was doing the same in the bathroom.

"But we'll question her…and also the hospital about this. I admit, it looks very strange and mysterious. Your poor uncle certainly doesn't need any more problems."

Before I even left the hospital, however, another very big problem arose…on my cell phone. It was Johnson again. This time he sounded more shook up than ever.

"Joe, where the hell is Owens?"

"Last time I saw him he was about to haul that elevator thug to the police station."

"He didn't quite make it. Both the police and our agents have tried to reach him since we're in a hurry to get that final story draft of your uncle's."

"All I know is that he has a cell phone and can let us know if he needs help. Charley McKay was with him."

"Well the worst scenario would be if the Elroy mob sidetracked him and now has that draft," warned Terry.

"If they have I'm sure they'll destroy it as fast as they can."

"Yeah…and they'll destroy the computer as well, just in case that copy was saved there," Terry noted.

"Geez—what a disaster. Our hope for evidence is kind of dwindling," I sighed.
"But I'm worried about Owens, Terry. The computer may have crashed but Owens also may have. God, they may try making an example of him…who knows what horrible things they'll do to him if they know he's spying on them."

"Have you contacted McKay? He may also be in trouble," asked Terry.

"I haven't yet…I figured he or the chief would call me if there's a problem, but that's before I heard Owens was missing."

"Charley may be also," said Johnson…"You'd better call the chief if you don't hear from McKay soon."

No sooner had I clicked off my cell phone than it jingled again—this time with the phone number of Charley. My gosh, he must have been reading my mind.

"Where are you at?" was about all I could say, anxious to hear what happened since I last saw him and Owens bringing the elevator hit man to justice.

"A car drove up as I was helping George put that guy into my squad. They had their guns out and forcibly pulled our prisoner and George into their car and sped off. I'm okay, although a bit shook up by all this. I couldn't shoot back since I had all I could do struggling with those hoods."

"Did they also take Al's papers? Hopefully George didn't have them with him," I asked with my fingers crossed.

"I didn't see any papers…but now that you mentioned it, he did have a file of papers or something with him."

"If they did, we may as well forget arresting Elroy. Al's story drafts were the most convincing evidence against him. I'm sure they already have his computer smashed into a thousand bits so no one can bring these up.

"And I understand from the DEA they couldn't find a disc on this anywhere. So I assume this is also in Elroy's hands and is probably ground up by now."

Charley tried to calm me by noting that there's many new computer upgrades now that perhaps can be used to help find the drafts, although admitting that without Al's password and the title he put on the drafts it would indeed be a struggle.

"Damn," he said in disgust, "If only I had noticed the license plate on that car that took off with George. Everything happened so suddenly."

"Well, let's hope George is able to break loose. Don't forget he's one smart guy and able to handle himself quite well," I said, also trying to keep my hopes alive.

After biting some more of my nails, and saying prayers now for both my uncle and George, I waited nervously and impatiently to hear good news about both. Recalling doctor Lahn's prognosis of Al's apparently good progress I thought at first it may be time to inform aunt Kay about this…but, then again, I decided to delay this for fear of a relapse or something else that may suddenly go wrong.

Realizing Elroy was now out to stop any and all obstacles in his way, I thought about my own family. Who knows, this guy may try kidnapping even Maddie or threaten Sarah to keep me from reaching his goals. I now wouldn't put anything past him and his henchmen.

This prompted me to phone Sarah on my cell phone. When the phone kept ringing for several minutes I could feel my forehead get sweaty. Just before clicking off in despair, however, the pretty voice of my wife was heard. "Joe, where the heck are you? I'm so concerned about you…a call came in just a few minutes ago. Wouldn't say who it was, but said for you to lay off the case you're on if you ever want to see Owens."

"Did you get their number on our monitor, or recognize anything about the caller?"

"No, he hung up immediately before I could say anything."

My God, I thought, they're using Owens as a hostage. I couldn't explain all this to Sarah but warned her to stay home, keep the doors shut tight, and don't take any more calls.

My next thought was to call the chief and alert him to all this. After all, he recommended Owens for this duty and perhaps can help figure out how to rescue him.

Besides, the chief should be updated on all that's been happening.

I assume by now chief Hermes has heard enough about Elroy and may want to rush right in and arrest him. But, then again, that may just increase the danger to Owens and maybe even Al. Also, Terry warned that there still may not be enough proof to make an arrest until we can get Al's story draft back that clearly and precisely tells about the councilman's involvement. All the rest seems based on assumptions and hearsay.

Weighing all the negatives and positives, I still decided the best thing to do is to contact the chief and also tell him about Terry's concerns. I knew the chief wouldn't want to cause any harm to Owens and Al and hopefully would carefully plan a strategy to help. I also kept in mind that he wouldn't want to make an arrest that wouldn't be supported by the best evidence possible. Who knows, this could backfire—and we both could be reprimanded and—worst yet, be reporting to Elroy.

My call to the chief is put on hold, as usual, and I know that if the precinct secretary doesn't answer soon I'll be listening to some gosh-awful taped music, interrupted by a recording saying: "Please hold…your call is important to us." My only alternative is to click onto my personal and very reliable secretary Liz. I got through to her at once and even before her usual greeting she quickly announced: "*You just heard from George.*"

"Are you sure? Last I heard he was missing."

"Well, wherever he is...he's okay. But he sounded all out of breath...left you a phone number to call. I tried contacting you earlier but you seemed to be always on your phone. He didn't have your cell number so I gave it to him, but he may not have the chance to use it...so please call the number he gave me ASAP."

Guess I'll have to lecture Liz again to get as many facts as possible from callers. However, I'm sure Terry would say I should be the last to scold anyone for that.

How in blazes could Owens get away to make a phone call to anyone? Unless perhaps he overcame his kidnapper. I kept in mind that he's a young, muscular fella who had some experience as a professional boxer...which was one of the reasons why our police department was interested in hiring him. But besides his welfare, I also was wondering about the status of Al's papers.

I pushed aside all these concerns and immediately began clicking onto Owens' numbers, knowing that he wanted me to immediately call him...hoping it isn't too late to catch him on my cell phone.

My first attempt to reach him got only static for mis-dialing. My second attempt caused moments of ringing—at least indicating it was trying to connect to him.

As I kept holding the phone, I glanced at my watch once more thinking time had nearly run out for Al—if indeed there's any left at all.

Finally I heard a rather nervous voice respond: "Owens here."

"George are you okay? This is Kavinsky—where the hell are you?"

"I was able to beat off my attacker, Joe, and am now heading toward our police precinct. But in the struggle that guy got away with the papers you gave me."

My first reaction was staggering...I just about dropped the phone hearing this, realizing now Elroy had the upper hand. By destroying the story drafts and smashing the computer nearly all hope was gone to assure damaging evidence that could jail Elroy.

But my mind saved me from calling off all these seemingly futile attempts at retrieving the drafts by reminding me of the possibility of a disc that Al may have made of his story, and that perhaps he hid it away in case it's ever needed in some emergency situation...such as this. However, I also recalled the DEA reported they couldn't find the computer disc, and aunt Kay said there wasn't any in his home office. I still hesitated calling Al's editor since it may indicate I was breaking my promise not to try to divulge anything about the Elroy matter yet.

"Are you bringing the attacker in?" I asked in hope of finding out where, and if, this guy may know where the disc might be.

"No, unfortunately in my attempt to get away he sped off without my getting even his license plate numbers. Sorry about that—I was too busy trying to recover from all this."

I shrugged this off, realizing that George was still very much a rookie in our detective department.

Suggesting that he should report in as soon as possible to the chief, I clicked off and began attaching my cell phone to my belt, but before I could finish doing this it jingled again. This time the call was from doctor Lahn. But what the heck could he want?...I was with him only a short time ago.

As usual he began by formally introducing himself: "Mr. Kavinsky, it is I—doctor Lahn." This time, however, his voice was trembling a bit. "I'm afraid I may have some bad news...it appears your uncle has taken a turn for the worse.

"He seems to slip from getting better to falling again into a coma. I am trying very hard to keep him stable. But it may be best if you and your wife and his family began to prepare to see him. I don't expect that he'll slip away...but perhaps it's best that you're around here for him."

I could tell by his voice that Al may not make it after all, and that having his family and friends with him may indeed be comforting for all of us—and perhaps for him. While weighing the pros and cons of alerting my aunt and wife, Lahn added another problem to ponder—this time regarding Marlis, the health care advocate.

He noted, "She asked me and the guard if it was okay if she could be at his bedside—knowing he's still in a coma she wished to say some more prayers for him.

"As you instructed, we denied her that at first. But she insisted and emphatically told us not to disconnect any tubes or do anything that would speed up his death, as though I ever thought of that. We allowed her to look at him, but then told her to depart."

"And did she?" "Yes, but only after using the restroom. She wasn't feeling very well, she said. She was there for only a few minutes and left the room after blessing Al again."

"Sounds like all went well...far be it from me to stop prayers for my uncle."

"But it hasn't—after she left I also used the bathroom. There was a bottle of common cold medicine she apparently forgot to take with her. I examined it thoroughly and found it contained pseudoephedrine—an ingredient that's also used to produce methamphetamine."

Chapter 28

Oh Lord, I thought, that's all that we need…another maker of meth in my uncle's room. Drugs seem to be running wild in there.

"But don't jump to conclusions Mr. Kavinsky," cautioned the doctor, "It may very well be she normally takes this when she's coming down with the flu—or something. But I thought it my duty to tell you about this…especially knowing you're a detective."

"Thanks doc, I won't. But I think I'll check into it and also call my aunt and wife as you suggested to let them know now is a very important time to be with Al."

However, I had to act calm and somewhat casual when encouraging them to come to see Al—as difficult as this may be. I didn't want to shock them into thinking it was definite that Al may be dying—although he may very well be. So I stressed that the doctor encouraged their visit believing it would be best for all concerned.

But my wife, who can 'read me' like a book, sensed that something was wrong by asking "Joe, what's up?—is he about to pass away?"

"Who knows? but just in case…it's best that we're all there. He needs some prayers. I'll see that the guard lets us all in. I suggest you and Kay hurry up It's sort of a three-way crisis now—whether he lives, dies or—God forbid—is already brain dead."

When I clicked off the phone, I felt mad at myself for going too far even with my wife in describing the serious and unpredictable situation with my uncle. She always had a way to seek the facts from me, making me sometimes wonder who the detective in our house really is. Maddie had some of these traits, of course like all toddlers—wanting to know "why" about everything and demanding answers.

However, no one, not even one of the smartest doctors around, seemed to have answers yet for saving my uncle. In utter frustration, I threw up my arms and walked out of the hospital to get away from all this depression. I was about to light a cigarette near the steps of the hospital when I noticed some guys carrying signs.

At first they looked like picket signs, probably carried by hospital help disliking how they're paid or treated. God knows, there's been a lot of nurses on strike lately…there's such a shortage of them I would think they have some great bargaining power. But when some came a bit closer I realized they were protesters and the signs they had became more visible.

In fact, I almost fell down the steps on seeing what they were protesting. All their signs stated: "FREE AL BENJAMIN!—UNPLUG THE LIFE TUBES-LET HIM DIE IN PEACE!." I couldn't believe what I was seeing. A bunch of tough looking sign carriers wanting to disconnect life from my poor old uncle—who I'm sure would be fighting right now to wake up and punch their lights out.

I had to restrain myself from running down the steps to take the signs away. There also were some jerks honking car horns in agreement as they drove past the phony protesters parading in front of the hospital.

Before I even came to the steps, however, I noticed someone who appeared to be the leader of this bunch. The more I looked, the more I could identify who it was. At least his cocky walk and arrogant manner seemed very familiar.

My God!...*it is him!*—it's John Elroy waiving to the demonstrators.

I waited for Elroy to come closer, he apparently didn't see me right away. When he did, his smile vanished suddenly. I almost poked my nose into his face and, with my fists clenched, asked—"What the hell do you think you're doing?"

"Whatever I'm doing is perfectly legal, Mr. Kavinsky. These folks have all the right in the world to be protesting against keeping Mr. Benjamin alive when all the medical help available can no longer do this. It's a pity and shame that he should go on like this."

Hearing that, I grabbed the councilman's collar, brought my fist near his nose and threatened: "Listen, and hear me good, Elroy...call off your hounds and leave my uncle alone or you're going to be the one needing life support."

"I don't know what you're talking about. I don't know any of these people, I only know they have a right to promote their beliefs. I also don't know your uncle."

"Oh, I believe you do...and he also knows you, and your dirty tricks."

Accustomed to verbal combat as a politician, the councilman simply stared at me with a smirk and countered: "It's one thing to accuse me, but another to back it up. For that matter, you'd better be careful with such unfounded accusations, they could be cause for a law suit Mr. Kavinsky."

"Besides," he added, "You don't have any evidence of what you're saying, and I'm sure you won't be able to obtain any." With that, he walked away in his pompous manner, continuing on to the hospital entrance. Before he reached the door I hollered, "Just stay away from my uncle's room Elroy." He retorted, "Don't worry, I wasn't planning to. I have many friends to see in this hospital."

I was all set to tell him to go to hell, which I'm sure he will anyway, but I was distracted by seeing my wife and aunt running to the entrance from the nearby parking lot. They waived as they dashed up the steps. Both stopped to hug me tearfully, as though they realized this could be their final visit with Al and, of course, their very last chance to say goodbye.

But I still kept hoping this wasn't a goodbye…and that Al will be able to survive and get out of that darn awful funk that he's been in so long.

I did a sudden about-face and led them to the elevator, knowing that by now I shouldn't have to worry about any attackers waiting there—although I did feel my pistol on my belt inside my coat just to make sure it's there. A veteran detective does this quite often every day almost by habit…encountering so many bad guys-it's a good habit.

We reached Al's floor quickly, without any incidences whatsoever, but when the doors opened who should be looking at me but none other than Terry Johnson.

"The guard informed me you were coming. The doctor told him to expect you and your wife and aunt. At least our guard had it right this time," he smiled.

"Is the doctor still there? And how's Al doing now?"

"I'll let him tell you, he seems to be in a more talkative mood. After that I'll also tell you something about our latest investigation of those suspects you informed us about…but we still need that information Al was writing up regarding the councilman."

Although Terry seemed cheerful, I knew we were both still deeply concerned about Al's condition. With my arm around my aunt, we walked quietly into his room.

Our somber appearance was exactly opposite to what we saw on Lahn's face as he still sat on a chair next to Al's bed and continued to closely observe him. However, instead of his usual serious look he was smiling as we walked in almost with heads bowed.

We were surprised but delighted by hearing him say, "I was hoping you'd come soon, your uncle seems to be getting better. His breathing has improved along with his heart rhythm. At this point I do believe he's coming around."

He motioned us over to the bed, indicating he wanted us to also look at Al who still lay quite motionless with all his many tubes still attached.

"Please…talk to him. I really believe he may hear you," the doctor urged. "Now's your opportunity to comfort him. It may help to bring him around. I've seen that happen with other comatose patients on the brink of recovery."

My aunt held his hand, kissed it and mumbled, "Hello Al…we're praying for you honey. Please come back to us as soon as you can. Please don't leave us. We miss you so much."

Sarah was next, also kissing Al and telling him how much we want him to get well. She also said little Maddie missed him—and all the good times she had playing tag with him. I was next, repeating some of these sentiments but also included mention of Elroy.

"Al, this is Joe, we know what happened to you. Elroy wanted to keep you from writing about him. We think we have the goods on him…but unfortunately don't have all your story drafts to help prove it."

Talking "business" wasn't what doctor Lahn preferred, however, judging from the frown he gave me. So I finished my brief remarks by also saying how much we hope he can snap out of this. With that, I thought I saw a little smile appear on my uncle's face.

The doctor's smile also broadened on seeing this and said, "He has a great uphill battle, folks, but I do believe he's able to make it…in fact, he may be recovering sooner than expected."

As reassuring as this sounded, however, we were all rudely interrupted from rejoicing by some sudden noisy commotion outside the room near the door where the guard is stationed. We could hear loud talking and arguing and couldn't figure out what was going on until the guard poked his head in and explained, "There's some of those protesters out here and I'm telling them to go away. No need to worry, I think I've got this under control."

Damn, I thought, Elroy said he isn't planning to come here—but his hoods came, probably hoping to at least interfere with the doctor helping Al—or even turning off. the rescue equipment. "Good, keep them the hell away from here!" I yelled at the guard.

However, for a moment I thought one of them eluded the guard and walked in the room, but when I turned around I saw that it was Terry. He touched his lips indicating he would be quiet and walked over to the bedside, sort of peering down at Al the way some mourners do at a corpse, I thought.

"No, he's still alive—and doing better," I whispered to him.

I could hear Terry softly saying "great!"

The doctor suddenly raised his arm as if to quiet us, put his ears to his stethoscope and after several minutes sat back and announced: "I think he's coming-to right now folks."

It was hard to believe, but Al's eyelids began twitching, as though he wanted to see what's going on around him.

Complete silence engulfed the room as Lahn continued to monitor Al's lifelines and listen intently to his breathing. The oxygen bag seemed to be functioning normal as well as the monitoring of his pulse. But I was still sweating and crossed my fingers in hope of never seeing that pulse line become a straight line. The monitor beeping kept going strong and, thank God, never faltered or show any signs of a problem. Not being a medical guy, I also kept looking at Lahn's expression to make sure everything's okay.

Chapter 29

No one said a word as the doctor, without indicating any problems, advised Sarah to prop up Al's pillow, so his head was now facing us in a normal way. Lahn also began removing a tube from Al's throat and nose. Good Lord, I thought, is Al really ready for this?

Terry, standing next to me, put his hand on my shoulder to give me a little show of support as everyone tried to remain calm and hopeful. After a few anxious moments we noticed Al's eye lids flickering some more. His face, once very pale, flushed a little and then as we stood in awe—and as Sarah gasped—my uncle's eyes began to open slowly.

Needing some assurance, I nudged the doctor and whispered, "Will he know us? and how will we know he's not brain damaged?"

"You'll know as soon as he fully awakes," replied Lahn without any sign of doubt. "If he speaks sensibly and recognizes some of you, I'd say he's going to be all right mentally as well as physically. His throat pulsations also indicate good brain readings."

Terry overheard this and tightened his grip on my shoulder, reinforcing me for better or worse. It took a few more minutes for Al to move his head toward us and then his eyes opened and stared at us quizzically. Kay couldn't restrain herself any longer and nearly shouted, "Al honey we love you, please stay with us…do you know where you are?"

My heart skipped when my uncle didn't answer. He just looked blankly at his wife and then at each of us. We still didn't know if he was brain dead. I felt it was my turn to say something.

"Unc (I've been calling him that since I was a kid)…it's me, Joey. remember all the good times we've had together. We ran some crooks to jail—you with your stories and me with my gun. Wake up Unc!…we've still got more work to do."

He appeared to be studying me as though still wondering who the hell I am before he responded. When he did, it was with a slight motion of his hand—as though beckoning me closer to him. I moved next to him and put my ear close to his in hope of hearing what he was trying to say. When he did move his lips the sound came out like a whisper. But what I heard only made me frightened that his mind may indeed be gone.

"Pen—get pen for driving…pen and purse," that's all he could say before closing his eyes and stopping his mumbling. No matter…it didn't make any sense to me.

Terry heard it, too, but at first just shrugged it off thinking Al must be delirious. For some reason he must be thinking he's writing something with a pen. Oh well, once a wordsmith—always a wordsmith, I reasoned. But as he kept repeating the words "pen" and "purse, Terry and I had to realize that the lack of oxygen may indeed have left my dear uncle brain dead.

Not really knowing how to respond to what seemed to be gibberish, but tying in with some of his confusing words, about all I could say to my frail old uncle was, "Yeah, I guess you can write with a pen." As far as driving, I couldn't figure that out at all, or how it connects with anything he's saying.

I turned to Terry hoping he may be able to interpret some of this. But he also just shook his head and looked at me as if to say Al's mind must be gone. I noticed he had his hand to his chin while Al was muttering apparently trying to study what was being said.

Doctor Lahn placed a hand on my shoulder. and said softly, "Your uncle will be going in and out of consciousness for awhile. It will take some time for him to really be coherent. His vital signs still look good so don't give up on him yet if he isn't making much sense. The mere fact that he's talking at all shows that he still has thought waves. At least he's not in a vegetative state."

My aunt and Sarah were still so choked up over all this that I purposely didn't want to talk with them at this time. Terry, however, beckoned me away from the bed indicating he wanted to tell me something. When we were far enough away to talk without being heard he asked me to sit down with him. I figured at first he was getting tired of standing and wanted to chat about what's going on. But he became quite serious, taking a pen from his shirt pocket as if planning to write me a note with it. But, instead,—he drew me a picture.

I couldn't help but wonder if Terry believes I'm so stupid he has to draw things out for me. When I tried interrupting him to ask what the heck he's doing, he raised his hand to stop me from interrupting and then pointed to the pen.

"Joe, I believe what your uncle may be trying to say is that his information on Elroy is contained in a pen drive."

"Are you nuts? How can all that story draft be pushed into a fountain pen?"

"It's high tech—a very special pen drive that provides everything you need for simple, portable data storage. I understand it can access files from most computers, such as Windows, Mac and Linux. I'm using one right now."

"But it writes and looks like just a pen."

"Yes, the bottom half is a high quality ink pen but the top half contains the data storage drive," said Terry removing the top from the bottom sections.

"My God, Terry, are you telling me that even though we haven't Al's actual story draft or a computer disc of it, we should be able to bring up all his incriminating writing by simply using what looks like this pen?"

"Exactly, but we're still at a lost…we have to first find that pen. Once that's done it's just a matter of inserting it into the right outlet of almost any computer to bring up the copy. Your uncle was using Windows…wasn't he"?

"I'm pretty sure he was, but I'm such a computer goof that I hardly know how to turn one on."

"As you said, Joe, I think your uncle is trying to tell us something about how to get that story copy of his that would finally get Elroy."

My DEA pal suddenly stopped talking, as though a light went on in his mind, and stated, "Damn, didn't your uncle mention a purse?"

"Yeah, he sure did, whatever sense that makes."

"It could make a lot of sense. Namely, someone with a purse is holding that pen, whether they know it or not."

"Well that's not narrowing it down much, is it? I said with a shrug."

Terry was more upbeat replying, "Well, in our small group here the only two with purses are your wife and aunt. For what it's worth, let's start with your aunt."

Before approaching my grieving aunt Kay I was cautioned by Terry not to divulge anything about why she should check her purse…but perhaps simply say I need a fountain pen to write something.

And both of us knew this was very much a long shot in trying to locate that would-be pen in her purse or Sarah's, if indeed there is one.

"It's a very slim chance, Joe. Both of them may be without a pen. We'll keep looking into other possibilities, however, also in many other ways. I know we're just guessing at this point—in hope that we're interpreting Al's strange words correctly.

"Also, if one of them does have a pen, bring it to me and we'll check it out. Neither Kay nor Sarah are suspects, of course. Who knows, both may have seen it in Al's office when they were there."

I was somewhat puzzled by Terry's logic, but figured he knew, and experienced, what he was talking about. Things like pens and pencils do tend to get picked up easily when their laying about, especially when you might need them.

I began strolling over to my aunt, who was still holding her purse. Despite her age, she had a fetish for bright, loud colors which explains why I could spot her attractive purse right away. She's a dapper lady who you might refer to as being quite 'cool.'

At first she was a bit startled by my sudden presence. I could tell she was deep in thought and prayers for her struggling husband. I pretended to be looking for something in my pockets and asked if she might have a pen I could use.

Aunt Kay as usual was very cordial and even smiled—as though welcoming a break in her sorrow. "I think I still have the one Al gave me just before he went in for surgery."

Rummaging through her purse seemed to take a long time. After a few minutes she glanced at Sarah and asked, "Didn't I give you my pen the other day when we were at the mall and you wanted to fill out a questionnaire to win a cruise?"

"Oh my gosh! I completely forgot about that. Sorry, I know it's rather precious to you…and sorry, too, that my name wasn't drawn for that wonderful trip."

As she was about to return the attractive pen I asked Sarah teasingly, "You weren't going without me, of course?" She put her hand on my shoulder saying, "Of course not silly—I also filled out one with your name, and neither one of us is going anywhere."

This helped to brighten up the gloom in the room. Sarah then opened her purse and after digging around in it came up with one of the most eye-catching fountain pens I've ever seen.

"Al calls it his favorite pen, and said it's very valuable. He kept close tabs on it and never allowed anyone to use it," Kay said feeling somewhat guilty. "I noticed it in his special locked cabinet as I was cleaning up his office, and was able to get the key and admire it."

To help cheer Kay up, Sarah added that she didn't use it. She found another pen in her purse for the cruise contest. "I just couldn't use such a pretty, expensive pen for a raffle ticket…glad I found my old one way down in the bottom of my purse."

"Did Al know you had this, aunt Kay?" I asked wondering about Al's mention of a purse in the confusing words he spoke to me upon awakening.

"Yes, but only just before his surgery…he gave it to me and said to guard it closely. I couldn't figure out why it was so important to him. I told him I'd conceal it in my purse."

While she was talking I was preparing for the sensitive part of this conversation—I gently asked "May I borrow the pen aunt Kay?"

She surprised me by handing it right over to me. "If there's anyone that will take good care of this—it's you, Joey. Al always regarded you as a top cop and a most reliable nephew." Sarah agreed, with her head on my shoulder and in a loving way said, "It's in very safe hands with Joey."

I could see Terry approaching and left Sarah and Kay for a moment. I wanted to show him my 'trophy', and when we got together in a corner of the room checked it out.

"Like I thought, Joe, it's what's known as a flash pen with storage drive. And it's password protected. Amazing what these computer geeks will think of next."

"Wow—when can we try it out in hope it comes up with Al's manuscript on Elroy?"

"As soon as we can leave this room" terry said, "but we must have Al's password—do you have that?"

"I never knew it, but maybe Kay does." My aunt must have heard me, since she approached me with a curious look as though wondering why her name was being mentioned. I asked her if she recalls Al's computer password, but she didn't, saying it was one of those "private" things he never mentioned to her. Knowing my uncle, I wasn't too surprised. He was always very secretive about what and how he's doing on writing projects, especially those relating to the criminal world.

My thoughts about this, however, were suddenly interrupted when I saw doctor Lahn beckoning me to Al's bedside, he was almost waiving urging me to hurry.

"Al wants to talk with you," Lahn whispered when I reached the bed.

Seeing my quizzical look, he added "Don't worry, my monitor shows his mind is okay, his oxygen is better, and he's getting more aware of what's happening. Try to listen to him. He asked for you."

Hearing this, which renewed my hope and made me smile, I bent closer to Al's moving lips. But was greatly disappointed when all I could hear were some goofy words sounding like "*Royalty*—get royalty."

I looked back at the doctor and asked, "What's he saying?...it doesn't make sense."

Before Lahn could respond, however, I heard some more sounds from Al...this time like he was trying to say "Joey...Joey!"

Although he was breathing hard and still mumbled a lot, he was even attempting to beckon me closer. When I pressed my ear almost to the point of touching his mouth I could hear him struggling to say something like—"royalty, pen...get royalty."

In fact, it almost seemed he was getting irritated with me by having to repeat this, as if he was being frustrated by my futile attempts to understand what he's saying.

I turned to Terry to try to help me understand. He was now also next to the bed and I'm certain could pick up on some of this strange conversation.

"He must think he's some sort of royalty...perhaps he may have been reading too much about king Charles and his new bride before all this happened," I said with a shrug trying to make light of a very sad situation.

Terry didn't respond at first, but instead just stood there with hand on chin again as if trying to also figure out what Al was trying to say. He stopped frowning after a moment or two, then kind of snapped his fingers, and acknowledged my comments in a rather studious manner:

"I don't think so, Joe. He may be trying to tell us his password."

He suggested, "let's piece together what he's said. "Al mentioned *pen* and *get* and then, even more curiously, *royalty.*"

"Yeah—so what?" I asked my veteran sleuth friend. "How in hell does royalty fit in?"

"By fitting the letters together, and when changed around somewhat they can come very close to spelling Elroy."

Looking at the frown I was giving him, Terry explained quickly:

"Don't you get it? Move the L to the front then add the ROY. That adds up to *LROY*—dropping, of course, the A.T and extra Y."

"But why would he make this so difficult?"

"Because he's your very clever uncle. He certainly wouldn't want to make it easy for anyone, especially that bunch of hoods who are after his story copy and trying to find the evidence he collected and wrote about regarding the councilman."

"If we need his email address, Terry—I have it, unless he also changed that to throw off his attackers."

"Perhaps—but everything now is a hunch. We're sort of just guessing at this point, Joe…and hoping. I suggest we get to a computer modem with that pen drive and, hopefully, use that 'put-together' password *royalty* to see if it all works out."

"For that matter, there's probably a modem around here that'll handle this—with so much need for computers among the office and medical staffs," I said—recalling the many work stations I've observed around this hospital area. "You mentioned that most computers now-a-days are equipped for this type of device."

Chapter 30

"Yeah, it should only take a few minutes to find if our hunches are right. All we need to do is put the pen drive into the special slot at the base of the modem, much like loading a CD Rom."

"And then what?" I asked due to my amateur knowledge for operating a computer as well as my poor understanding of computer lingo.

"And then with the computer on Microsoft Windows, or whatever word processing system this facility uses that's hopefully compatible with the drive, we should be able to bring up all of Al's story copy…and print it out."

"Terrific—'mister wizard' let's do it! I think there's a computer right around the corner on this very floor."

As we both hurried out the door, aunt Kay, Sarah and the doctor all looked in surprise wondering what was going on. The doctor adjusted his glasses to make sure we were leaving, stammered a little, and then returned his gaze on Al who appeared to be getting more awake and nearly had his eyes fully opened at this time.

Fortunately, it wasn't necessary to discuss what we're doing with those at the computer station since time was so crucial—and there was an unused computer waiting for us.

However, there was an unexpected obstacle when an elevator door near us suddenly opened. A tough-looking guy strolled out and headed toward us—with one hand inside his jacket. Being cops, we knew this could mean he may be holding a gun.

"What are you guys up to?" he demanded.

It's too late for us to try any self defense, if needed. He kept approaching and both Terry and I stood up expecting some big trouble. But at about this same time we heard the elevator door open again.

It's our man, George Owens!...with a gun and, unlike the big creep facing us—he appears all ready to use it.

Reacting quickly, Terry and I pounced on the suspected would-be attacker and were able to disarm him without much of a struggle. He indeed did have a concealed weapon—a loaded .38 revolver tucked under a belt next to his bulging belly.

We could hardly hear George trying to explain why and how he came to our rescue due to all the hollering and threats coming from the guy we're wrestling.

"As your 'inside man' with the Elroy group, I recalled they were planning to closely follow you in case they may still find a way to get that evidence your uncle obtained."

Chapter 31

He explained, "I've been tailing some of the hit men and followed this guy who was asked to interfere with anything you may be doing that could lead to Elroy's arrest."

"So, you've been riding the elevators again, George—like our last meeting at the hospital," I said grinning.

Thanking him for being so diligent, Terry and I continued holding down The guy on the floor. As he was being cuffed by Johnson, I began using my cell phone to notify my precinct that we'll be bringing him in for investigation. George agreed to take him to another area of the hospital to avoid having him witness what we're trying to do at the computer.

Terry, still sweating after all this, immediately returned to his attempts at using Al's mysterious password device as the thug was being led away. He carefully inserted the tip of the fancy pen into a slot at the very bottom of the modem once he had the word processing screen up. Al's password and email address were quickly accepted, and low and behold…up came all the incriminating copy my uncle had uncovered on that scheming councilman.

"My gosh, this goes on for pages and pages," exclaimed Johnson as he stared at the lengthy manuscript rapidly flowing before our eyes.

My first thought was God bless my uncle for having the determination and guts to take on that bastard despite all odds.

As I was taking pride in Al's accomplishment, my wife tapped me on the shoulder. Smiling broadly, she announced that Al was now awake and talking coherently.

Although knowing Terry had everything under control, I still felt obliged to ask him if it was okay to leave. He seemed very preoccupied, browsing over what Al had written, but found time to reply briefly."

"Fine! Go see your uncle and congratulate him for me. Geez—Al did a great job. Everything seems well documented to help prove our case against Elroy. With this in hand, Joe, there should be no trouble charging him with conspiracy, drug dealing and other criminal activities…and God knows what else.

"And we have what we need to arrest his gang of creeps who have been in and out of his room to keep him quiet." He added with that special grin of his, "In fact, we're probably rounding them all up right now."

Sarah and I almost ran back to Al's room, overjoyed that he was now out of his lengthy coma. When we arrived, he was not only awake but was sitting up in bed talking with the doctor and Kay.

Chapter 32

"Al, Al...welcome back!" was all I could say rushing to him. He was smiling and, although still quite feeble, extended his arm in greeting. "It's so great to know you're recovering from that overdose. We've been waiting for this for a long, long time."

His voice was much stronger now. "You and me both. I've been struggling to get out of that tunnel I fell into for what seems like ages ago. About every time I saw daylight I'd fall back into that swirling hole and drop to the bottom."

"But honey...you're safe now, we won't let you slip back in," aunt Kay promised still clutching her rosary and blessing herself.

"Thank God!—I can't describe what horror I went through. It was such a terrible nightmare," Al groaned. He looked at each of us surrounding his bed and added, "And thanks to all of you for helping me get through this."

"Special thanks should go to doctor Lahn here for coming to your rescue," I said, pointing to the doc as he stood with us and began to blush a little.

Lahn humbly acknowledged: "I'm thanked enough by knowing that your uncle has survived all this in such a good way. Believe me, it was touch-and-go for a very long time...and for awhile I wasn't too sure he'd come through at all."

I noticed Al starting to nod off, as though ready to fall asleep again, while everyone in the room was talking about his recovery. The doctor whispered to me that it often takes some time for overdosed patients to stay awake for long periods.

Knowing this, I made it a point to get very close to Al again to let him know we were able to use his password and got his Elroy story draft okay. When hearing this, he opened his eyes again, smiled, and said weakly: "Thank God, Joey, I hope you can put him away for good."

"Thanks to you, we'll be able to. I'm sure the cuffs are already being put on him and his gang—including Frenole, Marlis, that red head, etcetera, etcetera. You don't have to fear them anymore. They were going to keep you quiet forever."

"Good, just don't let me fall into that tunnel again. I was scared by the light below, but when I got close to that light above for some reason I wanted to reach it."

"I'm sure you did, however maybe God doesn't need a great reporter right now with him—but still needs you here to continue exposing the evil around us—an expert writer like you with a nose for news who can keep the truth from being smothered up." I could see Al suddenly get restless and nervous again. I also saw Terry leaving the room as our conversation turned so sentimental. Al seized my arm and pleaded: "But please, nephew promise me you'll never say that word again. I never want to hear it or even think about it."

"What word, Al?"

"*SMOTHER*"—he almost shouted. "I'm terrified at the mere thought…it makes me want to keep my hands up to guard against being suffocated by a pillow."

"Must be something you experienced in your coma. But then again—by accidentally knocking that phone off the hook on the table next to you with your hands you helped lead us to the happiness of your waking up." He sighed, "Happy indeed—but please also help me to never again see that tunnel, my old hands couldn't climb out of it again."

With his mention of hands, I grasped his to show support, knowing of course this is one situation—among many in this weird theatre of the unknown—that I nor anyone else can do anything about…not with guns, fists, threats, cops or DEA agents. Seeing my aunt, still with a rosary in her hands, I sighed and peacefully concluded that Al should leave this entirely in the special hands of the Lord. After all, as the saying goes: we're all *in the palm of His hands*. And I'm sure the Almighty has been holding Al securely, protecting him from the bad guys while enabling this apparent miraculous recovery from his longtime nightmare—and really handed him back to us.

While deep in thought regarding all this, and looking upward for some divine guidance, I was suddenly interrupted by a firm hand on my shoulder. It almost startled me.

In fact, I was nearly frightened to find out where that strong grasp was coming from. It was Terry's…he also began patting me on my shoulder as I bent toward Al to catch my uncle's every feeble word. The whole room had been rather quiet and somber until then.

But it was like clouds clearing and a rainbow appearing when my DEA pal announced—with that cockeyed grin of his—"I come with more glad tidings, Joe. You'll also be very happy to know that the chief just called to let you know that he's finally taking you off that crazy—and phony—tax case. And since Al's now talking, I was able to turn on his special tiny voice-activated recorder and get even more evidence that should help put those bad guys away for good."

THE END

978-0-595-37753-4
0-595-37753-X

NORMANDALE COMMUNITY COLLEGE
LIBRARY
9700 FRANCE AVENUE SOUTH
BLOOMINGTON, MN 55431-4399